An
Unwelcome
Proposal

Also By Bree

Historical Romance:

Suspenseful Contemporary Romance:

Middle Grade Adventure:

Paranormal Fantasy:

An Unwelcome Proposal

(#4 A Forbidden Love Novella Series)

by
Bree Wolf

An Unwelcome Proposal

by

Bree Wolf

This is a work of fiction. Names, characters, businesses, places, brands, media, events and incidents are either the products of the author's imagination or used in a fictitious manner.

Any resemblance to actual persons, living or dead, or actual events is purely coincidental.

Cover Art by Victoria Cooper

To my Beta Readers
Your Honest Words Mean the World to Me

Acknowledgments

A great big heaping mountain of thank-you to everyone who lend a helping hand in the development of this book: my family, friends, beta-readers, proof-reader, avid readers, feedback givers, reviewers, hand-holders, muses and many more.

To name only a few: Michelle Chenoweth, Monique Taken, Zan-Mari Kiousi, Tray-Ci Roberts, Vicki Goodwin, Denise Boutin, Elizabeth Greenwood, Corinne Lehmann, Lynn Herron, Karen Semones, Maria DB, Kim O'Shea, Tricia Toney, Deborah Montiero, Keti Vezzu and Patty Michinko.

An Unwelcome Proposal

PROLOGUE

England, November 1818 (or a variation thereof)

"Is something the matter, Marianne?" Christine asked, eyeing her friend critically. Usually cheerful by nature, her childhood friend seemed most distraught as she wrung the handkerchief in her hands with such strength that Christine feared it would tear in two any moment now. "You do not seem like yourself."

Marianne sighed, and her eyes, clouded and slightly red-rimmed, travelled to the window. "Everything is fine," she mumbled, but her shoulders slumped as though she didn't have the strength to hold herself upright.

Slightly exasperated, Christine took a deep breath, her eyes narrowing. "Even if I were blind, I'd now that something was wrong." When Marianne glanced up, Christine leaned forward, holding her gaze. "Tell me what has you so distraught."

"Truly, it's no—"

"Marianne!"

Sighing once more, her friend swallowed, her eyes drifting back and forth between Christine and the twisted handkerchief clutched in her hands. "Peter has been…" Shrugging her shoulders, Marianne sighed yet again.

Christine felt the desperate urge to slap her. When cheerful, Marianne was a delight to be around. However, when something was wrong, Christine preferred to avoid her. Clearly, that was no longer an option!

"Do you want me to guess?" Christine asked, sounding as exasperated as she felt. "However, it would save us both some time if you simply told me what is going on."

Not looking up, her friend began to pick at the handkerchief's embroidery. "He's been distant lately."

"And?"

Marianne shrugged. "Sometimes I feel as though he's avoiding me," she mumbled, eyes fixed on a small, embroidered rose bud. "He goes out, and when I ask where he's been, he…" Again, she trailed off.

"You believe him to have an affair," Christine stated matter-of-factly.

Instantly, Marianne's eyes flew open in shock and her jaw dropped down before she clamped it shut once more, defiance in her clear blue eyes. "How dare you suggest such a thing?"

Shaking her head, Christine looked at her friend indulgently. "You suggested it, dear Friend. However, it was I who had the courage to say it out loud."

"Peter would never—"

Christine snorted. "Are you suggesting that men generally do not have affairs? Or that your husband is above such matters?"

Swallowing, Marianne turned her attention back to the handkerchief.

"Did you ask him?" Christine pried although she already knew the answer.

Slowly, Marianne shook her head.

"Why not?"

Again, Marianne sighed. "I'm afraid of what he'll say."

"Isn't it better to know the truth," Christine asked, "than to be left wondering?"

When her friend refrained from providing an answer, Christine took a deep breath. Married for less than a year, Marianne had been deliriously happy only a few weeks ago. To see her in such misery now once more proved to Christine that marriage was not a desirable state for anyone. Even those who entered into it with love in their hearts would one day wake up and find it gone. Slipped out in the middle of the night.

What followed then was heartbreak and humiliation, at least for the female half of the population, whereas men generally sought to distract themselves by entering into an affair. Christine had observed so more than once and had long since come to the conclusion that a husband would not do for her.

However, taking a lover was something that she seriously began to consider.

If only she were a man and could do so without worrying too much about her reputation. At least, her father's generous foresight ensured that she would never be without means.

"What should I do?" Marianne's feeble voice jarred Christine out of her own wonderings.

Christine shrugged. "Discover the truth," she advised, "and then find a way to live with it." After all, what else could she say? Marianne was Lord Fythe's wife, and until the day of his demise, her choices were, therefore, severely limited.

A knock on the door saved her from saying anything further that might hurt her friend's feelings. "Enter."

Stepping into the parlour, her father's butler bowed to her, a silver platter in his hand holding a sealed envelope. "I apologise, Miss, but this was just delivered. The messenger said it was urgent."

"Thank you," Christine mumbled and reached for the letter. As she recognised the seal, her heartbeat quickened, and she flipped the letter open, her eyes eager for the words hastily scrawled on the page.

Dear Miss Dansby,

I apologise for the manner of this communique, however, time is of the essence. I formally request your presence at Harrington Park.

"Merton," Christine called over her shoulder. "Have my things packed immediately. I'll be leaving within the hour."

"Is something wrong?" Marianne enquired, her face pale as her eyes glanced at the letter in Christine's hands.

Ignoring her friend, Christine read on.

13

My brother, William, has been thrown, and as he has yet to regain consciousness, your sister, as you can imagine, is beside herself with worry. Therefore, I'd be much obliged if you could travel to Harrington Park post-haste.

Yours sincerely,

Wesley Everett

CURSE YOU, WESLEY EVERETT

As the carriage rumbled along the snow-covered road, Christine tapped her right foot on its puddle-splattered floor. Glancing out the window, she tried to guess how much longer it would take for them to arrive as her eyes drifted over the heaps of snow to her left and right. Once more she cursed the timing of such an emergency!

Taking a deep breath, Christine forced her foot to still. However, the tension coursing through her body like a live being caught up with her before long, and too soon she found her foot tapping the floor at an even accelerated pace. Gritting her teeth, her fingers curled into the thick fabric of her overcoat.

In her mind, she saw her sister's face, tear-streaked and pale, sitting at her brother-in-law's bedside, his eyes closed and his body still.

Catherine had always been the more delicate of the two sisters, and yet, a hidden strength rested beneath her soft nature, and Christine hoped that she would not despair.

Despite her own misgivings of marriage in general, Christine knew of the deep love that lived between her sister and her brother-in-law.

With her own eyes, she had watched them fall in love in a single night, and although she had sought to caution her sister, she had been unable to ignore the tender devotion that connected the two. On their wedding day, Christine had prayed with all her might that Catherine and William's love would last, that they could be counted among only a handful of fortunate individuals, who never lost the glow that came to their eyes upon beholding the other.

Never had Christine contemplated the thought that Catherine would lose the love of her life to an accident. Of course, such things did happen, however, …

Shaking her head, Christine once more glanced out the window, wondering where they were. With trees, bushes and meadows covered in snow, she could not even guess at their location. For the millionth time, Christine pulled the letter that had sent her on this troublesome journey from her reticule. As her eyes once more flew over the lines as though hoping to find something she hadn't seen before, Christine swore under her breath.

"Curse you, Wesley Everett," she hissed. Could he not have elaborated? Told her more than the few scrawled words that were neither here nor there?

Picturing his dark brown locks and piercing blue eyes, she wondered what he would say if she were to trade a polite greeting upon her arrival for a forceful smack to his cheek. Would he be stumped? Or would he grin, a devilish twinkle in his eyes as though he had expected no less of her?

Wesley Everett truly was a strange man. He had this annoying ability to make her blood boil with anger with a single look or curl to his lips. Everything he did felt like a challenge, and Christine wondered what it would feel like to see him again for the first time after her sister's wedding day.

Had he grown to be even more insufferable in her absence? She could only hope he'd stay out of her way. With her sister in desperate need of comfort and guidance, the last thing in the world that Christine needed was a man like Wesley Everett getting in her way.

Leaving his brother's bedchamber, Wesley took a deep breath and for a moment rested his back against the heavy wooden door. Nothing!

His brother still remembered nothing of the past five years. How was this possible?

Again, Catherine's tear-streaked face drifted before his eyes, and he cringed at the desperate longing he had seen in her gaze. What would she do if William never remembered her? If he never remembered his wife? The woman he loved?

Shaking his head, Wesley started down the corridor. He ought to make certain she was all right. After she had fled her husband's chamber the day before, he had not seen her. His mother had told him that she was fine considering the circumstances, but still Wesley felt the need to see for himself.

As he approached the door to her chamber, it suddenly opened and with her back to him, his sister-in-law stepped out. Moving silently, she reached for the door handle and quietly pulled it closed.

A frown on his face, Wesley watched her. "Catherine? Are you all right?" Then she turned, and his heart jumped into his throat.

"Chris," he whispered as he took in her smoky green eyes and full lips. A devilish grin came to her face as she beheld him and her eyes narrowed. Like a predator, she took a step closer, her eyes never leaving his face, and his heart began to hammer in his chest.

"I didn't know you'd already arrived," he said, clearing his throat, as he watched her approach. Still, she remained silent, her eyes trained on his, a calculating gleam in them that sent chills down his back. In response, his own gaze narrowed, and he saw the tension that held her, her right arm quivering ever so slightly. "Are you all right?"

Coming to stand before him, she took a deep breath.

For a moment, he felt himself relax before she suddenly drew back her arm and her hand connected with his cheek a split second later.

Flinching, Wesley reached up and touched a hand to his burning cheek, annoyance chasing away the more delicate feelings that had seized him upon seeing her. "Are you mad, woman?" he snapped, rubbing his cheek, as his eyes searched her face. "Why did you do that?"

"Because you're an idiot!" she snapped, poking an accusing finger at his chest. "How dare you send me such a letter?" Her eyes blazed with fire. "I was beside myself with worry, not knowing what was happening and how dire things were. Could you not have elaborated?"

Shaking his head, Wesley stared down at her. "And that's why you slapped me? That's hardly a reason!"

"It's a bloody good reason!" Stomping her feet, she glared at him. "You halfwit! You inconsiderate—"

"I wrote what I could under the circumstances," Wesley defended himself. "As I said time was of—"

"Of the essence," Christine finished. "Yes, I know. Still, you couldn't have taken two minutes? Two minutes?" Shaking her head, she looked at him with a hint of pity in her eyes as though he was someone of low intelligence who couldn't possibly have reached such a conclusion.

Taking a slow breath, Wesley swallowed. "I admit I probably could have been a little more detailed," he forced out, and a triumphant sparkle came to her dark eyes.

Her voice, however, sounded sincere as she spoke. "Thank you." Brushing down her dress, she took a deep breath, and the tension left her shoulders. Looking up at him, she asked, "How's your brother?"

Wesley sighed. "Not good." Gesturing down the corridor, he fell into step beside her as they headed toward the large staircase. "He still does not remember anything," he said, glancing at her. "I assume Catherine's told you."

Christine nodded. "She did. She's devastated." As they descended the stairs to the ground floor, she looked at him. "How can he forget years of his life? I've never heard of such a thing."

"Neither have I," Wesley admitted, waiting for her to enter the front parlour before stepping in himself. "Dr. Martin says that he has heard of such cases. However, they are extremely rare."

Seating herself on the settee, Christine shook her head. "There's no treatment, is there?"

"No." Taking the armchair across from her, he met her eyes. "I don't know what to do. I see the pain they're in, and yet,…" He shrugged.

"I know." With her lips pressed together in determination, she nodded. "We'll think of something." Again, she nodded as though to convince herself. "We will."

A soft smile came to his lips at the gentle devotion that shone in her eyes. She was a fierce woman, one not to be trifled with, and yet, she was loyal to a fault.

"Tell me about him." Holding his gaze, Christine nodded in encouragement. "When he woke up, was he aware how much time had passed?"

"No, to him, it was still May 1813," Wesley explained, remembering his brother's pale face. "And when I told him, the truth hit him like a ton of bricks."

"And he doesn't even remember meeting her?"

"No, for him, it's as though he has never laid eyes on her in his life."

Closing her eyes for a moment, Christine sighed. "We need to do something."

"Do you have a suggestion?" Wesley asked, a hint of incredulity in his voice.

Christine's eyes narrowed. "Not yet," she snarled, regarding him with open perusal. "Answer me this, dear Brother-in-law."

"I'm not your brother-in-law."

Ignoring him, she continued. "Will you just stand by and watch them lose the life they've loved? Or are you willing to do whatever it takes to ensure that their story will have a happily-ever-after?" A challenge in her eyes, she watched him, and Wesley couldn't help but feel uneasy about her question. Deep down, he knew that whatever her mind would concoct would be something rather unwise, and yet, he could not ignore her plea for help.

Holding her gaze, he nodded his head. "Whatever you need."

A soft smile came to her lips, and she leaned back, relaxing against the cushions. "Even if he does not remember her," she said, determination in her voice, "he fell in love with her once, he will again. They may not get back the past they shared, but at least they'll have a future."

Remembering the pained expression on his brother's face, Wesley frowned.

"What is it?"

"You weren't there," Wesley began. "When Catherine came to him after he woke up, he looked at her as though expecting his memories to return instantly. Even more than that. I think a part of him hoped that he would see her and know her to be the woman he'd loved." Wesley shook his head. "And when that didn't happen, he could barely look at her. Although he does not remember her, it pains him to see her in such misery. Under such dire circumstances, how are they ever to fall in love again?"

For a long moment, Christine held his gaze before her eyes became distant, and he could almost see her mind at work.

After the accident, Wesley had sent word to her because he'd thought Catherine could use the comfort of her sister's presence. However, sitting across from Christine now, a surge of hopeful expectation went through him, and he realised that somewhere deep down he had hoped that her mind would succeed where his had failed him.

Even if her plans could usually be categorised as insane, at least, any plan—as insane as it might be—would be better than none.

After a small eternity, her eyes returned to look into his and a mischievous smile curled up her lips. "I have an idea," she whispered, and Wesley took a deep breath, bracing himself for what was to come.

2

A LUDICROUS PLAN

*L*eaving her sister's bedchamber, Christine turned to look at Wesley. Admittedly, he looked somewhat pale after their talk with Catherine. "Are you all right, Wes?" she asked, hoping that he hadn't changed his mind. After gaining her sister's approval, Christine had thought nothing stood in their way.

He shrugged. "There still are a few aspects of your plan that have me concerned," he admitted, his eyes barely meeting hers.

Christine tensed. "Because it's *my* plan?"

"That doesn't matter," he said flatly, walking past her.

Riled at his dismissive attitude, Christine strode after him. "If you do not believe it will work," she snapped, stepping in front of him so that he had to stop in order to avoid running into her, "then why did you agree to it in the first place."

"Because it's the only plan we have," he snapped. His eyes, however, held an amused twinkle as his gaze slid over her.

Gritting her teeth at the slight shiver that ceased her, Christine once more poked her finger in his chest. "Don't humour me, Wesley Everett. If you believe my plan to fail, then tell me so here and now!"

"I have doubts," he admitted as his piercing blue eyes held hers. "After all, this is a serious matter. Whether we succeed or not, we will be deceiving my brother."

"For his own good," Christine countered.

His eyes narrowed, and he lowered his head to hers. "He might fail to see it that way." His eyes held hers, and he took a deep breath. "No one likes to be deceived."

Holding his gaze, Christine swallowed as his warm breath caressed her skin. "Do not tell me you believe that your brother would not readily agree to anything that would ensure a future with the woman he loves!"

Considering her words, Wesley stilled. "Assuming he is still the same man he was before."

Christine frowned. "Of course, he is."

"People change," Wesley counselled. "Sometimes it takes a long time, and sometimes it happens in the blink of an eye."

Confused, Christine held his gaze, feeling as though he was no longer speaking about his brother. Something had changed between them. Christine was certain of it. Before, he had not looked at her the way he did now, had he? If he had, she had not noticed.

But she did now.

"At our core, we are who we are," Christine said, ignoring the fluttering sensation in her belly. "William loves her, whether he knows it or not. And once he does fall for her again, he will not mind the means by which it was achieved. If it makes you feel any better, I will take complete responsibility for what is to happen."

A soft smile curled up the corners of his mouth. "Is there anything you wouldn't do for your sister?"

"I love her," Christine whispered, feeling the sudden need to take a step back. "She is my other half. I cannot be happy if she is not as well."

He chuckled. "Are you saying you're doing this out of pure self-interest?"

Enjoying the banter in his tone, Christine smiled. "Don't we all." Raising her eyebrows in challenge, she said, "Selfless deeds do not exist. We all do what we do to ensure our own happiness. Fortunately for those we love, it is always dependent on theirs."

"This is an adventure to you, is it not?" Wesley asked, eyeing her curiously. "You did not solely suggest that your sister take on your identity to allow her to converse with her husband without the pressure of expectation, did you?"

Grinning, Christine said, "Of course, it was my prime reason. However, a girl can enjoy herself, can she not?" He took a slow breath as his gaze lingered on hers, and Christine felt the need to speak lest he... "Although I must admit that the thought of giving up my wardrobe pains me greatly."

A low chuckle escaped his throat. "I dare say it is not the wardrobe that will give you away."

Her eyes narrowed. "Do you not believe I can act the proper lady?"

"Act? Maybe." The corners of his mouth drew up in amusement. "Be? Never."

Shocked by his boldness, Christine felt her hand itch with the need to slap that smug smile off his face. "Wesley, Everett, how dare you—?"

"Calm yourself," taking a step back, he glanced at her hand, "and know that what I said was meant as a compliment."

"A compliment?"

"It most certainly was. After all, who would want to be proper when the opposite promises to be a lot more entertaining." Winking at her, he turned on his heel and walked away.

Left behind, staring at his receding back, Christine was at a loss for words—a rather rare occurrence, she had to admit. Had he just suggested something indecent? Although his words had been far from explicit, the look in his eyes had spoken of hidden desires; desires that echoed within herself. He had always been handsome, however, now, he possessed the annoying ability to throw her off balance with his mere presence.

Considering her own outlook on life, Christine realised that he might be just the right man for her. After all, he seemed just as disinterested in marriage as she was herself.

A slow smile came to her lips as she contemplated the idea of making him a rather indecent proposal, one that would surely wipe that smug smile off his face.

The right time would come, she counselled herself, and then it would be her turn to throw him off balance—literally speaking, of course.

The next few days Wesley spent by his brother's bedside.

Doomed to rest, William's mood grew foul. He had little patience and more than once threatened to simply stride from his bed and do as he pleased. Only Wesley's careful reminder of the life he did not remember could keep William where he was.

Again and again, his brother asked about his wife, about the way they'd met and the life they'd led. And although Wesley did his best to answer his brother's questions, he did not wish to say too much, knowing that it was imperative William speak to Christine...or rather Catherine pretending to be Christine.

Had he actually agreed to this insane plan?

Whenever he would come upon Christine, his heart would pick up its pace as though he had been drugged, and he had trouble forming a coherent thought. Had she always been this intoxicating? There was something about the fire that burned in her dark green eyes that set his whole world ablaze.

And she knew it, didn't she?

Sometimes, he thought to see a knowing twinkle in her eyes, and he felt certain that without the constant reminder of why they both were currently at Harrington Park, he would have already whisked her away to Gretna Green.

When Dr. Martin finally gave his permission for William to leave his bed, there was no stopping him. Although apprehensive, he strode from his room that night, his eyes gliding over the home of his childhood, seeking to detect the small anomalies that time inevitably brought with it. However, before long, their conversation just as inevitably returned to the one topic that brought pain to his brother's eyes: Catherine.

"I'm sorry to put this on you, big brother," Wesley said, a touch of guilt seeping into his heart, "but you need to know how difficult this is for her."

Misery clearly edged into his features, William turned away. "I know."

"Do you?" Wesley pressed, following the plan Christine had concocted in that beautiful, and yet, foolish head of hers.

"What do you want me to say?" William snapped as he spun around. "I feel as though you're accusing me of forgetting her on purpose."

At his brother's outburst, Wesley instantly regretted his words. What was Christine doing to him? Had he completely abandoned sanity? "I'm sorry. That is not what I meant to say. I simply thought to explain that she is beside herself with sadness and that it might take some time for her to face you, to speak to you." At least, that much was true.

"I understand."

If only he did, Wesley thought, but instead said, "We should go. Supper will be served shortly."

Upon entering the dining room, Wesley felt his brother stiffen. Toward the other end of the long table stood their mother as well as the two sisters, who turned toward them upon their approach.

Seeing Christine dressed in a proper, mildly coloured dress, her eyes lowered and her hands wringing a handkerchief as though distraught, Wesley could barely contain his amusement. And yet, he had to give her credit for she did look truly saddened. He could only hope that William would not see through their charade.

Introductions were made quickly, and before long, they were all seated around the large table, an uncomfortable silence hanging over their heads.

Occasionally, Wesley conversed with Catherine, seeing the strain their charade caused her clearly on her face. After all, was she not also a victim of Christine's ludicrous mind?

Glancing down the table, Wesley saw an equally tormented expression on his brother's face. Christine, however, seemed to be enjoying herself. While her whole demeanour could be considered appropriate for a woman in her position—or rather her sister's—there was something in her eyes that spoke of enjoyment rather than dread. Whenever he would catch her gaze, Wesley could see a hidden excitement gleam from underneath her proper exterior, and his own pulse quickened at the mere thought of it.

Only his brother's desolate state could keep him from enjoying that evening as much as she did.

3

WHOSE BROTHER-IN-LAW?

"Look!" Christine called over from the window front. "He's going after her!"

Excitement bubbled over, and she bounced up and down on her feet, her eyes glued to something in the gardens.

Coming to stand beside her, Wesley saw his brother follow Catherine down the snow-covered path into the back garden that was laced with tall-standing hedges.

"Oh, this is going exactly as planned!" Clasping her hands together, Christine gnawed on her lower lip, her eyes sparkling like the snow crystals outside. "And you thought it was a foolish plan," she accused him, slapping him on the arm in unabashed triumph.

Wesley gritted his teeth. Something about the way she spoke always riled him into contradicting her. For some reason, he could not allow her to be right. "Your enthusiasm is a little premature, don't you think?"

Forcing her eyes from the scene outside, Christine fixed him with an icy glare that sent Wesley's heart into an uproar. Why was he enjoying this so?

"Your negativity serves no purpose," she hissed, once more poking an accusing finger into his chest. "If you intend to contribute nothing but poignant comments, you might as well take your leave." She turned back to the window. "Don't worry. I'll take care of them."

Wesley scoffed, surprised how much the thought of leaving her side affected his mood. "I would be a fool to leave this ludicrous endeavour in your hands without at least making certain that all is done to ensure its success—as unlikely as it may be."

"Unlikely?" Christine echoed, her voice indicating that she had clearly taken affront. Inhaling deeply, she turned to him once more, and her dark eyes roamed his face as though trying to understand him. Did she know how much he enjoyed their banter?

Holding her inquisitive gaze, Wesley inhaled her intoxicating scent and his hands itched to reach for her. Only the code of proper conduct that had been drilled into him since birth prevented him from throwing caution to the wind.

"You are a wolf in sheep's clothing, are you not?" she whispered, her eyes serious as a knowing curl came to her soft lips. "You seem proper and well-behaved, always courteous and considerate," she observed, her eyes sliding over him in open perusal, "but that is not who you are underneath, is it?"

Stunned into silence, Wesley stared at her. Never had a lady spoken to him like this nor glimpsed his true nature as easily as Christine.

"You have a wicked sense of humour," she continued as though reading an indictment. "Although you are loyal and respectful of those you care about, you often find yourself wishing you weren't forced to abide by society's rules and could simply do as you please. Is that not so?"

Wesley drew in a slow breath. Then he took a step forward, and her eyes widened ever so slightly as she raised her chin to hold his gaze. Looking down at her, Wesley gritted his teeth as his gaze travelled down to where her teeth worried her lower lip. "You surprise me, my lady. I thought a proper young woman such as yourself would find the company of a man such as you just described more than a bit alarming. However, you do not seem worried in the least."

A slow smile curled up her lips. "I never said I was a proper lady. I do try to act the part—I suppose for the same reason you do—however, underneath I believe I'm a lot like you."

Frowning, Wesley opened his mouth to reply. However, a shout from outside interfered.

Instantly, their heads snapped sideways, and Christine almost pressed her nose to the glass as she stared out into the garden. "They're having a snowball fight," she exclaimed, joy ringing in her voice. Then she turned to look at him, new triumph shining in her eyes. "As unlikely as you believe it to be," she taunted, "I think your brother has just taken the first step of falling in love with Catherine all over again."

Ignoring the look of decisive superiority on her face, Wesley watched as William and Catherine chased each other around the garden, throwing and evading snowballs as they went. At the sight, some of the tension left his shoulders, and Wesley hoped with all his heart that his brother would once more come to love the woman he'd married.

In addition, that would free his mind to contemplate much more tantalising ideas that had only recently entered his mind. Glancing at Christine, he wondered what she would say if he truly were to act as he pleased.

A part of him thought—and feared—that she might not even object.

Seeing the joy on her sister's face, Christine felt her own heart dancing in her chest. Catherine's eyes glowed as she told them about the morning she had shared with William in the snow, and her voice reverberated with hope, hope that one day her husband would come to love her once more.

Foolish plan? Christine thought with satisfaction as she remembered Wesley's remarks from that morning. Eyeing him with disdain, she turned back to her sister. "So, what's next?"

"What do you mean?" Catherine asked, a frown coming to her face.

"Well, we need to create opportunities for the two of you to be together," Christine said, determined to proof to Wesley that her mind was capable of more than thinking of the latest fashion, "preferably alone. We cannot leave that to chance. That might take too long."

Stepping closer, Wesley cleared his throat, and Christine felt his presence as he came to stand to the side of her left shoulder as though he had touched her. A shiver went over her, and it took all her will-power to remain unaffected. "While we're on the subject," he spoke, and his breath tickled her cheek before he stepped around and looked at her, "have you considered leaving?"

"Leaving?" That was the last thing she had expected him to say.

Wesley nodded. "The estate, I mean. I imagine your presence here is less than…beneficial." The mischievous twinkle in his eyes stirred her resistance, and had it not been for her sister's presence, she would have gladly slapped that smug smile off his face once more.

"But where could she go?" Catherine asked, oblivious to the undercurrent in her brother-in-law's tone. "And for what reason? As his *wife*, she belongs at his side."

Rolling her eyes, Christine sighed. "Well, I could always have an ailing friend in need. I will simply talk to Will and tell him that I received a message from a friend begging me to call on her."

Holding her gaze for a moment too long, Wesley nodded before he said, "I suggest that we involve as few people in this as possible. Tell Will what you said," he turned his gaze to Catherine, "and then I will take her to Sanford Manor."

"Sanford Manor?" A dim recollection of her sister telling her of the snug little house somewhere in the middle of nowhere entered Christine's mind, and a shiver went down her back. "What on earth would I do there?"

A barely suppressed grin on his face, Wesley said, "Stay out of the way," before he turned to Catherine. "I'll take her to Sanford Manor. As you know, it's a small estate with only a handful of servants, and as long as she stays in her room, that shouldn't pose a problem."

"Excuse me!" Christine demanded, eyeing him with a hint of suspicion. He was enjoying this too much, and the crinkles around his eyes clearly told her that he had an ulterior motive. Although her heartbeat quickened at the thought of his ulterior motive—whatever it might be—she refused to be manoeuvred across the chess board like a pawn.

If she couldn't be the queen, she'd rather not play at all!

"Only," Catherine hesitated, a touch of unease drawing down her brows, "will it be proper for you to escort her to the estate without a chaperone to accompany you?"

Instantly, an idea flared to life, and Christine stepped forward and took her sister's hands, elbowing Wesley out of the way in the process. "Do not worry, dear Sister. People will have no reason to gossip. After all, he is my brother-in-law."

As expected, she could almost feel Wesley tense up behind her. A low rumble escaped his throat, and he almost growled, "I'm not your brother-in-law. I'm *Catherine's* brother-in-law."

Forcing an earnest expression on her face, Christine turned to him, delighted to see obvious displeasure edged into his blue eyes. "And since I'll be Catherine, you'll *be* my brother-in-law, understood?"

Gritting his teeth, he swallowed as his eyes burned into hers, a promise of retribution flaring to life.

Goose bumps broke out all over Christine's body as she held his gaze, grateful for the layers of fabric that hid her own traitorous reaction to his presence. Then she allowed herself a little, triumphant smile, which had him turn on his heel and stride over to the window, before addressing her sister once more. "Don't worry. You'll be fine. Me, on the other hand, will suffer greatly."

"Are you worried about your reputation after all?" Catherine asked, her face betraying the concern she felt.

"Oh, aren't you a dear?" Christine chuckled. "No, I'm worried about being locked up in a small country estate for one reason alone, and that is boredom."

A low growl reached her ears from the window front, and Christine could only hope that Wesley Everett was far from the gentleman he always portrayed. After all, boredom was the last thing Christine hoped to find at Sanford Manor.

4

OFF TO SANFORD MANOR

Watching the footmen load their luggage onto the carriage, Christine drew her sister aside. "For once, do not worry," she counselled, gently squeezing Catherine's trembling hands. "Just be yourself. Laugh and smile and live as you always have with all your heart and soul, and he will remember you. I promise."

Blinking back tears, Catherine nodded. "Thank you for everything," she whispered. "I know this is terribly inconvenient for you, and I can only hope that you will find something entertaining to do at Sanford Manor."

Suppressing a grin, Christine smiled. "Do not worry about me, dear Sister. I have every intention of finding amusement wherever I can." Turning to William, she whispered a tearful goodbye and allowed him to assist her into the carriage.

As he stepped back, Wesley walked up to him and gave him a brotherly embrace. Glancing at them, Christine wondered about the knowing grin that spread over Wesley's face as he said something that had William's eyes open wide.

Then he stepped back, and with a last nod for his brother, Wesley took his seat in the carriage.

"What did you say to him?" Christine asked, unable to contain her curiosity any longer.

Meeting her eyes, Wesley smirked, and for a moment, she thought he would not tell her.

However, as the carriage rumbled along, slowly inching down the drive, a deep smile spread over his face. "I told him that I knew he remembered something."

Christine's eyes went wide. "And did he?"

"I'm certain of it," Wesley confirmed. "Yesterday, when you told him about our departure, he looked at Catherine with such longing regret that I could barely contain the relief I felt. He didn't want her to go, which became all the more obvious when you informed him of Catherine's intention to stay behind and aid him in his recovery."

Clapping her hands, Christine bounced in her seat as warmth filled her heart. "How wonderful!" she rejoiced before her eyes met Wesley's, open triumph in them. "I knew it! Maybe we should have made a wager."

Wesley laughed. "And what would you have wagered?" A smirk came to his face as his eyes slid over her, and for a moment, Christine feared…or rather hoped…that he would suggest something improper. "The contents of your closet? Although what I'd do with alluring gowns I could not say."

Glancing down at her simple overcoat, hiding a gown that was just as simple underneath, Christine huffed in annoyance. "Maybe we should have wagered about our destination," she suggested, and a gleam came to her eyes. "Maybe it's not too late to wager." She raised her eyebrows in open challenge.

Grinning, Wesley shook his head. "I'm afraid I have to decline. Even if you believe otherwise, I have more sense than to enter into an impromptu wager with a woman whose motives remain unclear."

Christine laughed. Had he always been this entertaining? "You insist on Sanford Manor then?"

"I'm afraid I have to. After all, our siblings' happiness is at stake."

Rolling her eyes, Christine sighed. "We've done all that we could by leaving. Where we spend the time of our absence is irrelevant."

"While you may be correct with regard to William's feelings for Catherine," Wesley stated, his gaze unwavering, "I believe it to be unwise to add to their troubles by causing rumours. You," he fixed her with a determined gaze, "ought to stay out of sight. Therefore, Sanford Manor is perfectly suited to our needs."

"Our needs?" Christine asked, biting her lower lip.

Suppressing a smile, Wesley ignored her. "It is far off the main road, and the only neighbour within reach is an old friend of ours. Therefore, we are in no danger of being discovered. Apart from the servants employed at the manor, no one will know you're there."

"Do you intend to tell them who I am?"

Frowning, Wesley hesitated. Clearly, he hadn't made up his mind yet.

"After all, I'm not a blood relative of yours," Christine reminded him, and the way he met her eyes told her that he was very well aware of that fact. "Would the servants not spread rumours as well? Would people not be surprised to hear that Christine Dansby is staying at two places at once?" Grinning at him, Christine wiggled her eyebrows.

Wesley took a slow breath, a hint of exasperation in his eyes. "I've not yet made up my mind," he admitted, clearly uncomfortable at not having thought everything through as well as he thought he had. "As far as I know Catherine has been to Sanford Manor only once for a couple of days, and that was months ago. Maybe the servants do not remember her all that well, which means that you can easily pass for her."

Christine frowned, enjoying the way he fidgeted in his seat. "But would it not be strange for my sister to be spending the weeks before Christmas alone in a remote manor with only her brother-in-law to keep her company?"

As his jaw clenched, Wesley inhaled deeply through his nose, his eyes narrowing as he regarded her.

"You have to admit that I'm right."

Almost imperceptibly, his head bobbed up and down. "Do you have a suggestion then?"

"You could tell them I'm your mistress," she blurted out before her nerves could fail her.

Wesley's eyes bulged. "Excuse me?"

Ignoring the touch of heat that burned in her cheeks, Christine nodded. "You have to admit it makes the most sense."

"Does it?" he growled, shock evident in his clear blue eyes. "How so?"

Christine once more rolled her eyes at him. "Please, Wes, you are a man of the world. Do not pretend that you do not know what I'm talking about. Tell me this: what would society think of a woman who accompanies an unrelated man to his country estate without at least a chaperone?"

Wesley's brows drew down as he regarded her with curiosity.

"You know I'm right," Christine challenged, delighted with the dark tension that had come to his posture. It made him seem wildly dangerous. Willing her heart to slow, she held his penetrating gaze. "We can give them a fake name, and I will make certain that any resemblance between me and my sister is as little as possible."

Swallowing, Wesley cleared his throat. "Are you not worried about your reputation should anyone find out who you truly are?"

Christine shrugged. "Was it not you who suggested Sanford Manor for the very reason that it was off the main road?"

"While the probability of being discovered is remote," he huffed, "it is not non-existent."

Christine laughed. "Are you afraid you could be pressured into marrying me?"

His eyes narrowed. His lips, however, curled up into a small smile.

Unsettled for a second, Christine rushed on. "If you are, allow me to put your mind at ease. I have no intention of ever marrying…anyone. I assure you this is not a clever way to trap you into marriage."

If possible, his eyes narrowed even more as he regarded her with curiosity. "Is that so? Well, then I suppose there is no reason to think of another explanation, is there?"

A relieved smile came to Christine's face. "Not at all. I'm glad you agree with my line of reasoning. After all, it's irrefutable."

Wesley chuckled. "You are an unusual woman, Christine Dansby."

"Is that supposed to be a compliment?"

"I haven't decided yet."

Cocking her head to the side, she glared at him. "Be that as it may. At least, my explanation promises a little excitement." A smile on her face, she bit her lower lip. "I've never been anyone's mistress before."

Again, his eyes bulged, and he stared at her as though she had just sprouted another head.

When the carriage drew up to Sanford Manor, it was already late at night. The snow reflected the few dim lights shining in some of the downstairs windows and thus allowed for a vague impression of the small manor house. Judging from the expression on Christine's face, it was worse than she had expected.

"Stay in the carriage," Wesley instructed once it had pulled to a stop. "I'll speak to Thompson—"

"Who?"

"The butler." Glancing out the window, Wesley heaved a sigh of relief when the front door remained closed. Clearly, they had not been noticed yet. "I'll speak to him," he continued, turning his attention back to the woman sitting across from him, "and inform him of," he gritted his teeth, slightly cringing at the words to come, "let's say, the nature of our relationship." At what point had he completely abandoned sanity and agreed to this? "He will instruct the rest of the household to stay out of our way as much as possible."

"That seems like a good idea," Christine agreed. However, a good idea by her standards was probably still a bad one.

After waving away Thompson's apology for not having prepared for his arrival, which of course he couldn't have considering that they hadn't given him any notice, Wesley informed him of the delicacy of the situation.

With each word, Thompson's countenance grew darker, and try as he might, he could not hide his displeasure from his master. "I'll have the rooms readied immediately and a warm supper brought up…my lord."

Clearing his throat, Wesley nodded. He couldn't blame the man for his disapproval; after all, Wesley could not say why he had agreed to Christine's suggestion in the first place. Was it truly because it had been the most reasonable explanation? He desperately wanted to believe so. However, he had to admit the thought of her as his mistress was most intriguing.

Escorting Christine into the house, Wesley noticed with relief that no curious eyes and ears were lurking in the shadows—at least as far as he could tell. "This is to be your chamber," he stated, stepping into the largest of the upstairs bedrooms. Anything less would have probably sent her back out into the night. As it was, she merely crinkled her nose and surveyed her new surroundings with a touch of displeasure in her dark green eyes.

In that moment, Wesley felt the desperate desire to simply lock her in this room and only return for her once the situation at Harrington Park had been resolved with satisfaction—however long that would take.

As it was, that was not an option, and so he gestured for his trusted coachman to deposit her trunks in a corner of the room before closing the door behind him. "I must ask you to stay in this room," he implored, eyes searching hers, hoping that she would understand the gravity of the situation after all. "Everything you require will be brought up to you."

Christine huffed, incredulity clouding her eyes. "Surely you're jesting."

"May I enquire what you are referring to?"

Stomping her foot, she fixed him with an unwavering glare, her hands resting on her shapely hips. "Allow me to make one thing clear, my lord. I refuse to spend my time at Sanford Manor in this shoe box of a room."

Gritting his teeth, Wesley shook his head. He was merely trying to protect her. Why would she make this so difficult?

Holding his gaze, she shook her head once more. "I will not."

"How can you—?" he broke off before he would say something unwise. Raking his hands through his hair, Wesley stomped toward her, eyes searching her face, desperately trying to understand the strange wanderings of her ever arguing mind. "You do understand that come morning the entire household will believe you to be my mistress, do you not?" he hissed, waiting…hoping…searching for a sign of shock—a slight widening of the eyes, a touch of red colouring her cheeks—any sign truly that suggested she understood the gravity of the situation they found themselves in.

However, Christine merely shrugged. "Is that not what we've agreed to?" she asked, an amused curl to her lips.

Wesley growled under his breath. If he didn't know any better, he'd think she was doing this on purpose. Squinting his eyes, he stared at her. Did he know any better? After all, he had only met her a mere two years ago and scarcely laid eyes on her ever since his brother's wedding day. How was he to know what kind of a woman she was? Had his instincts truly led him astray?

Wesley recalled that he, himself, had stated that she was far from being a proper woman. However, he had spoken in jest and not meant it in the most scandalous way.

"You seem troubled," Christine remarked, her smoky green eyes searching his face as she stepped closer and laid a gentle hand on his arm.

Wesley swallowed. What had he gotten himself into?

Although different in disposition, the two Dansby sisters were of a respectable family. Never had Wesley heard anything untoward mentioned with regard to their conduct. Neither out loud, nor whispered behind their backs. And although Christine was far more forthright compared to her younger sister, she knew the rules of society and obeyed them, willingly or not. At least as far as he knew.

"Wes," she whispered when he remained silent. "Is something wrong?"

Feeling the soft weight of her hand on his arm, Wesley took a slow breath, seeking to clear his thoughts. If only for his peace of mind, he needed to clear the air and address the unspoken issue between them. "I assure you I mean no disrespect," he said, gathering his courage to ask a young lady such an intimate question, "however, I feel obliged to enquire..." He took a deep breath as his heart hammered in his chest. Never in his life would he have thought that a woman could make him feel this way.

Inexperienced. Foolish. Immature.

"Yes, Wesley," she whispered, her breath a caress as it brushed over his lips, inevitably drawing his eyes down to hers.

Clearing his throat, he swallowed, forcing his gaze back up.

In answer, the corners of her mouth curled into a knowing smile before she once more bit her lower lip, a hint of shyness in her eyes. Could this woman be any more contradicting?

"Allow me to ask," he began once more, "do you...? I mean...you do not object to being considered someone's mistress as any proper woman ought to, which leads me to wonder whether you...eh...I mean, you're not...You haven't...?"

"I am no one's mistress," Christine stated in a calm voice, all hint of shyness vanished, "nor have I taken a lover. At least, not yet." The last part she added as though it were merely an afterthought. *Oh, no, it doesn't rain. At least, not yet.*

"Not yet?" Wesley croaked, his own voice barely more than a stunned whisper as he stared at her sparkling eyes.

Christine fixed him with a chiding look in her own. "Would you judge me for taking a liberty you demand for yourself simply because I'm a woman?"

Opening his mouth to answer—although he had no idea how to reply—Wesley couldn't get a single word out before she interrupted him.

"You yourself are still unmarried," Christine observed, her dark eyes looking into his, "and yet, I assume you are not unaware of the ways between a man and a woman."

"I..." Wesley stammered as heat shot up his neck, and he thought his face had to be glowing like a beacon in the dark. Blinking, he stared at her, uncertain whether his ears had deceived him.

"Do not deny it for it's written all over your face," Christine continued, her own cheeks merely having a rosy touch to them. "Would you deny me that experience?"

"Not at all," Wesley replied possibly a bit too hastily. Averting his gaze for but a moment, he cleared his throat. "As long as it is with your husband."

Christine snorted. "As you've only lain with your wife?" Calmly raising an eyebrow, she held his gaze. However, the rapidly beating pulse plainly visible in her graceful neck bespoke of the emotions hiding under her composed exterior.

For the millionth time that night, Wesley cleared his throat. "That is none of your concern."

"Then it is neither any of your concern who *I* invite into *my* bed."

Shocked beyond comprehension, Wesley took a step back as his world slowly became unhinged, bit by bit, with every word she spoke. "I'd ask you not to leave this room," he repeated, unable to process the myriad of information he had just received. "I bid you a good night." Then he turned on his heel and strode from the room, hoping against hope that he was already asleep and all this was merely a bad dream.

5

A MOST UNWELCOME PROPOSAL OR TWO

taring out at the snow, Christine cursed under her breath. Two days had passed since their arrival. Two days that she had spent sitting in her room.

Alone.

Since the night of their arrival, Wesley seemed to be avoiding her. Although he had promised to serve as her entertainment—which had sounded so promising at the time—something had frightened him off. Had she been too forthright? Did men not appreciate women who…?

Again, Christine cursed under her breath. She was a renowned woman of the world, well-versed in every area of life. She was well-read, intelligent and even more so she rejoiced in those attributes and prided herself on her accomplishments. However, in this one area, she was a novice. Never had she had the courage to venture into the unknown and explore the secrets reserved for the marriage bed with a willing man of her acquaintance. Despite her own reasoning, she had always been too uncertain of herself and had shied away in the last moment.

However, with Wesley, it was different.

With him, Christine felt as though she could be herself. She had been so certain that he would approve of her outlook on life and welcome her rather unusual proposal. A proposal, she had to admit, she hadn't quite but into words. At least, not explicitly.

Had he understood her meaning? Judging from the look on his face, he had. But why had he been so shocked? Did he not find her desirable?

Christine shook her head. No, that could not be it. For some reason that eluded her, he had been scandalised by her words. Surprisingly so.

Pacing the length of the room, Christine contemplated what to do next. If she allowed Wesley to have his way, she'd spent her entire stay at Sanford Manor—however long that would be—confined to her room. That thought made her physically ill and was, therefore, not even worth considering.

"Bloody hell," Christine cursed and having made up her mind strode toward the door and yanked it open. At least, he had not gone so far as to lock it.

When she found the corridor to be empty, she ventured from her bedchamber without a second thought. Realising that she had no idea which room was Wesley's, Christine pulled open the first door on her right, only to find it empty.

After two more failed attempts to locate him, the soft echo of booted footsteps echoed to her ears, and without hesitation, she proceeded to the other end of the corridor. Throwing open the door, she barged into the room.

"What the—?" Spinning around, Wesley froze as he beheld her. His hands dropped from the cravat he'd been attempting to tie. "What are you doing here? This is highly improper."

Laughing, Christine threw the door closed. "Don't you dare!" Hands on her hips, she strode toward him, eyes ablaze with fury.

With a frown drawing down his brows, Wesley turned to face her. "Is something wrong?"

Inhaling through her nose, she seethed with anger at his feigned ignorance. "You promised!" she snarled.

"I promised what?"

"To keep me company!" Shaking her head, she stepped in front of him, her hands trembling with barely contained rage. "I haven't seen you in two days! I haven't seen *anyone* in two days! I feel as though I'm going crazy!"

His eyes shifted to the door before they returned to her, and he took a step closer. "Would you lower your voice?"

Staring up at him in disbelief, Christine felt the last string of her patience snap. Without conscious thought, her hand flew forward, sailing toward the left side of his face.

However, instead of allowing her the satisfaction of slapping him, he caught her wrist in mid-air. An amused curl came to his lips then, the first sign that something other than indifference rested under his unconcerned exterior. "I'm deeply sorry for upsetting you," he teased. "Had I known the depth of your displeasure, I would have…"

"You would have what?" she challenged, welcoming the sudden rush of emotions that invaded her body.

"I would have…" As though distracted, his eyes trailed lower and for a second lingered on her lips. However, before Christine could seize the moment to her advantage, his head snapped up and he cleared his throat. "I would have recommended a good book or two," he finished lamely, belatedly realising that his hand was still wrapped around her wrist.

As though she had struck him, he released her and stepped back.

Disappointed, Christine took a deep breath, trying to focus her thoughts. "I napped today."

A frown came to his face before he simply said, "Good."

"Good?" she demanded. "Good? I'm not an old woman! I don't nap!" Shaking her head, she began to pace around the room. "Do you even know why I napped? Not because I was tired. No, that at least would have been acceptable. No, because I was bored out of my mind! Do you hear me? Bored out of my mind!" As an afterthought, she added, "I've never been bored in my life."

"I'm sorry," was all he said as he stood there, the mask of indifference back on his face.

Seeing red, Christine stormed toward him.

Apparently aware of the murderous gleam in her eyes, he lifted his hands in appeasement.

However, fuelled by two days of immobility, Christine could not contain her anger. With her hands balled into fists, she attacked him, pummelling his chest.

For a brief moment, he did not stop her. However, when her efforts increased, he once more grabbed her wrists. "What do you want me to do?" he snapped, lowering his head and looking into her eyes. "We are both stuck here for the time being. After your infamous revelations, I was merely concerned for your reputation."

Gritting her teeth, Christine stared up at him, annoyed by his pretence to care only about her reputation when she knew it to be a lie. Determined, she raised her chin. "My reputation is in no danger, *my lord*," she whispered. "After all, you're my brother-in-law."

Instantly, his eyes narrowed, and she could see the muscles in his jaw tense up. "I'm not your brother-in-law," he growled as his hands closed more tightly around her arms, and with one quick yank, he pulled her against him.

Christine gasped in surprise before a delighted smile curled up her lips. "Why does it upset you so that I consider you my brother-in-law?"

"Do you?" he demanded, his eyes drilling into hers, as he forced her arms back, wrapping her in a tight embrace.

Standing pressed against him, Christine felt the confinement of his hold on her with each shaking breath she took. "If you answer my question," she teased, "I promise I'll answer yours."

Again, the muscles in his jaw tensed as he took a slow breath. Then, to Christine's utter disappointment, he released her arms and stepped back. "Considering the position you're in at the moment," he growled out, his eyes shifting around the empty room, "it is ill-advised to…to tempt…" Shaking his head, he broke off and walked over to the window.

Following him, Christine felt her heart thudding in her chest. "To tempt you?"

He didn't reply.

Determined to have her answer, Christine stepped around him, squeezing in-between him and the window. "*Are* you tempted?"

Drawing in a sharp breath, he swept his eyes over her face and down her body. "Do you even have to ask?"

Christine smiled. "Despite my outspokenness, I am not well-versed in…these matters."

"Then why did you…?" He swallowed and shifted on his feet, leaning closer. "What do you want?"

"Did I not make that clear?"

"Abundantly so," he admitted, and his hands rose to settle on her waist. "Only I cannot believe what I'm hearing."

As she felt the heat of his hands burn through the fabric of her dress, Christine's breath quickened. "Why not? Is it not enjoyable for women? Or are women not *meant* to enjoy it?"

His hands slid farther up her back. "Do you even know what you're saying?"

"Well, as far as I've heard—"

"You've heard what?" His hands pressed her closer to him as his eyes searched hers.

Feeling her heart hammer against her rib cage, Christine forced herself to remain calm. She was so close. So close. If only... "If you truly doubt the source of my information—"

"How could I for I know nothing of it?"

"—then why don't *you* advise me yourself?"

His eyes narrowed before they dropped to her lips. "Advise you?"

A slow smile came to her mouth as Christine placed her hands on the arms that held her. "Show me," she whispered, seeing the temptation she was offering in his eyes. "Show me, Wes." Glancing at his lips so close to her own, she pushed herself up on her toes. "I dare you."

Although his hands tightened on her, she could see the struggle between desire and duty in his eyes. Swallowing, he lowered his head, his warm breath caressing her skin.

Christine closed her eyes. However, the moment she expected to feel his lips on hers, he tensed.

Instantly, her eyes flew open.

With his jaw clenched, he stepped back, shaking his head. "This is not right."

Exasperated, Christine cursed his name. Then, before he could turn around and walk away, she stepped forward and quickly closed the distance between them. "But it *feels* right, doesn't it?" Reaching up, she pulled him down to her, claiming the kiss she'd dreamed of since the moment their paths had crossed again so unexpectedly.

A part of her had been afraid that he would withdraw, that he would stop her, but he didn't. Instead, after a brief moment of hesitation, he responded to her tentative kiss with a hunger she had only glimpsed underneath his controlled exterior.

Unable to help himself, Wesley kissed her back. He knew he shouldn't. He knew it wasn't wise. Far, far from wise actually, and yet, here he was, almost crushing her in his arms as he devoured her lips like a starving man. What on earth was the matter with him? He could not recall ever having lost control like this.

Nonetheless, a part of him wondered why he even cared. After all, had it not been her who had dictated the terms of their relationship? Was he not giving her exactly what she desired? Why should he have scruples of taking advantage of an innocent woman when she was all but begging him to do so?

Mistress.

That one word echoed in his mind, and he almost cringed at the disrespectful and slandering connotation associated with it.

In his eyes, if anything, Christine was the personification of loyalty. Without a second thought, she had come to her sister's aid, doing her utmost to cheer her up and raise her spirits. Granted, she had a quite unique way of doing so. However, as unconventional as her methods were as true was her desire to guide Catherine and William back to their happily-ever-after. In order to achieve that, she was willing to risk her own reputation—for although she pretended not to care, Wesley doubted that she was being completely truthful on the matter.

For two days, she had sat in her bedchamber, and for all her threats and complaints, she had never once made good on them. The moment she had barged into his room, he had seen the strain on her face, annoyance so pure edged in her eyes that it had felt like a slap in the face to him, and he had instantly felt guilty for subjecting her to it. She had been right to lash out at him. After all, he had made her a promise.

Holding her in his arms, Wesley realised with a sudden shock as though a bucket of cold water had been poured over his head that her well-being mattered to him more than his own enjoyment. Being the younger, slightly irresponsible brother—the brother people generally didn't expect much of because he was not the one to inherit the title—Wesley had never quite experienced the tender feelings of protectiveness that suddenly began to bloom in his heart.

How ironic that it was to happen now when she was the last woman in the world who would ask it of him. She didn't want his protection, his name, his devotion…and love. She merely wanted his body.

And for the first time in his life, Wesley wanted more, needed more. Was he not worthy of love? Of being loved as the only man in a woman's life? The only man in Christine's life?

Breaking the kiss, Wesley stepped back, his eyes searching hers as he caught his breath. Determination hammered in his heart like never before, and from one second to the next, he knew exactly what he wanted. "Marry me."

At his words, the delicious smile that had curled up her lips vanished, and she stared at him as though he had just made an improper proposal—quite on the contrary.

Swallowing, Wesley tried to ignore the sinking feeling in his stomach and held her gaze, willing her to see the sincerity of his words.

However, when her hands fell from his arms and she stepped back, his heart sank and he knew that a long battle lay ahead of him.

"I don't understand," Christine said, her smoky green eyes searching his as though he had spoken in riddles. "I thought I'd made myself perfectly clear. I thought you, too, wanted nothing more but..."

Gritting his teeth, Wesley shook his head. "You cannot even say it, can you?" he challenged, seeing her answer in the slight blush that came to her cheeks. "You want me in your bed, and yet, you cannot even say the words."

Clearing her throat, Christine raised her chin. "It is not easy fighting the manners that were drilled into you since birth," she snapped, defensiveness glowing in her eyes. "Women are not supposed to..." She swallowed, unable to finish the sentence.

"And yet, you want to be someone's mistress." Taking a step forward, Wesley held her gaze. "My mistress."

"I never said *mistress*," Christine defended herself. "I only suggested it as a way of explaining my presence in this house. However, apart from this charade, I have no intention of being *anyone*' mistress, just as I have no intention of being someone's wife. I am my own person, and I will not lower myself to being someone's anything. I will not be an accessory that a man can pride himself on acquiring." Huffing, she stomped her foot. "I wanted to be...," she took a deep breath, "lovers. I want to be to you what you are to me. Equals." Taking a deep breath, she swallowed, then took a step closer, a soft curl to her lips. "What is wrong with enjoying one another for as long as possible and parting ways when passion wanes?" Running her hands up his chest, Christine pulled him closer, once more moulding her body to his.

Drawing in a sharp breath, Wesley felt his own resolve waver as her lips closed in on his. She *was* correct. This *did* feel right. At least, his body argued that it did. His heart, however, thought it deserved better.

"I cannot do this," Wesley spoke against her lips, cursing himself for this sudden and rather unexpected onslaught of conscience. Gritting his teeth, he looked down at her, a part of him unable to believe that she would truly reject him.

With disappointment shining in her dark green eyes, Christine stepped back. "I'm sorry to hear that."

Fearing the gap that would inevitably open between them, Wesley slung his arms around her, pulling her back against him. Holding her gaze, he said, "I care about you, Chris. Over the past two years, you've often been on my mind. Often quite unexpectedly. I've compared many a woman to you and found them lacking."

A slight blush came to her cheeks as she averted her eyes, uncharacteristically shy for an outspoken woman like her.

"I admit I do want to possess you," he said, and her gaze snapped up, narrowing. "I want you to be my wife, mine alone. I want to know that no one else will ever have a claim on you."

Shaking her head, Christine chuckled. "I never thought you to be such a fool, Wes."

"What?"

"Certainly there are exceptions," she admitted, "but in its essence, marriage breeds liars. Because of a spur of the moment, you tie yourself to another, and from that day on, you're trapped. People might not always realise it right away, however, the day comes when all passion is gone and the rest of your life looks as bleak as a rainy day." A hint of pity rested in her eyes as she looked at him. "And then you have to make a choice: accept the prison of your own making and live by its rules or break free and deceive those around you in order to feel…something…anything."

Frowning, Wesley stared at her. "I never knew you saw marriage that way. I never would have thought…After the way you supported Catherine and William, I—"

"She's my sister," Christine interjected. "I want her to be happy, and he was what she wanted. But do not believe that I did not counsel her to do otherwise." A gentle smile came to her lips. "But she is not me. We all have to do what we feel compelled to."

"What was it that gave you such an awful idea of marriage?" Wesley asked, remembering the cold cordiality that had always existed between his own parents. "Your father and mother always seemed…"

"Content?" Shaking her head, Christine sighed. "To this day, they care about each other. They always have. There is no dislike or animosity or even hate between them. They are…content. But that's it. They've both lost their chance for love and passion a long time ago."

Feeling utterly defeated, Wesley asked, "But what about marriage that begins with love?"

Her eyes narrowed as she regarded him with open curiosity.

Wesley swallowed, yet unwilling to explore how deep his feelings for her went. "What about Catherine and William's marriage?"

"As I told you," Christine replied, "I sincerely hope that they are the exception. I wish them all the best, but I fear that the odds are against them." She sighed. "I thought you thought of marriage as I do, as a hindrance, a limitation, something to be avoided at all cost." Searching his eyes, she smiled. "I thought you were my perfect match."

Touched by her words, and yet, knowing how she meant them, Wesley shook his head. "Whether the word is *mistress* or *lover*, I'm afraid it is not enough for me. For even pretending that you are my mistress turns my stomach upside down. It is demeaning, and so is *lover* as far as society is concerned…although I do agree that it centres on a more enjoyable aspect of the relationship." A soft grin came to his face as his eyes held hers, and for a moment, he thought to see deep sadness in them.

Then she blinked and forced the corners of her mouth back up. "What a pity," she said, feigned cheerfulness in her tone. "And here I thought my search had finally come to an end."

Wesley frowned. "Your search?"

"Well, if you're unwilling to…," she bit her lower lip and an embarrassed grin came to her mouth, "…share my bed, then I'm obligated to continue my search for a more willing gentleman."

Involuntarily, Wesley's arms tightened around her. "Any willing gentleman does not deserve the word."

Christine chuckled, a hint of amusement back in her eyes. "Well, as I have already found an unwilling gentleman, I can tell you that he won't do."

As the muscles in his jaw clenched and unclenched, Wesley held her even tighter, fearing that she would slip away if he released her.

"What are you saying?" he growled out, knowing exactly what her answer would be.

"I thought I'd made my intentions perfectly clear," Christine repeated as her hands slid up his arms. Despite the playful tone in her voice, her eyes remained serious as they gazed up into his. "I will not be made a liar," she whispered, "and so I will not promise something I cannot guarantee. How am I to know what will live in my heart in ten years or in twenty? Truly and honestly, I can only speak for right now, and that is all I have to give and all I expect in return."

Drawing one calming breath after another into his lungs, Wesley found himself close to losing his mind. Wrapped in his arms, the woman he...Christine stood before him, boldly telling him that she would invite another *gentleman* into her bed should he refuse her.

Never in his life had Wesley felt so utterly at a loss.

"The thought of you with another man turns my stomach upside down," he confessed.

A satisfied smile curled up her lips. "Then there's a simple solution."

"There's not." Shaking his head, he took a step back, loosening his hold on but not releasing her. "I do not want to live in fear for the rest of my days, dreading that one day when you find yourself bored by my presence."

"Don't we all?" Christine asked. "After all, although many people tend to believe so, marriage is not a guarantee for happiness. Maybe being aware of the possibility to lose someone will motivate us not to take those we care for for granted. Maybe there should be no guarantees. Maybe idleness is love's slow death."

Wesley swallowed. Although he had to admit that there was some merit to what she said, he could not fight that deep desire to make her his and declared it to the world once and for all. If only there were a way to change her mind. "You never truly had any objections to coming to Sanford Manor, did you?"

Biting her lower lip, she met his eyes. "Do you believe I lured you here to seduce you?"

"That thought has crossed my mind, yes." A tentative smile came to his lips as he regarded her. She was a beautiful woman, and her quick wit was incredibly stimulating. Around her, he felt more alive than ever, and the thought of spending a single day without her sent cold shivers down his back. "I will not just step aside and let you walk out of my life," he said, finally releasing his hold on her. "I want you."

Watching her, he saw the sparkle of mischief and humour leave her eyes, replaced by an awareness that almost brought him to his knees. "Know that I will not walk away."

Breathing heavily, she held his gaze for a long time, the intensity in her eyes building until it became too much and she finally turned away. "Nevertheless," she said, stepping toward the door, her eyes anywhere but on his, "I would ask you to respect my decision."

Stepping up to her, he whispered in her ear, "I respect that it is your decision. However, I will do my utmost to change your mind." As his breath caressed her neck, a slow shiver swept over her before her shoulders snapped back and she forced herself back under control.

Then she turned to face him, a forced smile drawing up the corners of her mouth. "Do what you must," she dared him and then strode from the room.

Staring at the closed door, Wesley felt as though he had spent the better part of the day hiking through the country side. Physically and emotionally exhausted, he sank into the large armchair by the fireplace, his eyes distant as he replayed the last few moments.

Ultimately, it all came down to one *simple* problem: the woman he…Christine was dead set against marriage.

But was that truly the problem? Wesley wondered. Would a woman in love ever under any circumstances reject the man she loved? Did that ever happen? Was the problem not that she did not want to marry, but that she did not want to marry *him*?

Considering that he had not yet declared his own feelings to her—which he hadn't even admitted to himself—her apprehension might not be quite as unexpected as he had thought. Maybe all he had to do was declare his feelings. But would that be enough? Maybe it would only be the first step on a long journey to win her heart.

Raking his hands through his hair, Wesley frowned.

He had never set out to win a woman's heart. How did one go about it?

6

STANHOPE GROVE

ith trembling hands, Christine closed the door to her bedchamber, then rested her back against it and closed her eyes.

It didn't help.

Still, she saw Wesley's smouldering gaze in her mind's eye, felt his breath on her skin and heard his words of affection ringing in her ears.

Why would it bother her so that he cared for her? After all, didn't she care for him as well? Naturally, he was her brother-in-law. Well, not quite, she corrected herself. However, he was family, and she was fond of him.

Very fond.

Gnawing on her lower lip, she willed her hammering heart to calm down. Had it only been the thought of sharing his bed that had unsettled her so? Did she have second thoughts after all? Although she had to admit that a certain nervousness had seized her the moment he had, she had enjoyed his kiss far too much. Not for a second had she thought of changing her mind.

For the first time in her life, Christine was unable to reason herself out of a situation and spent the rest of the evening pacing her chamber, tormented by questions she couldn't bring herself to ask, let alone attempt to answer.

Sleep proved restless as well, and she spent most of the night tossing and turning. Toward the second half of the night, however, she fell into a deep slumber, and before long, dreams flitted before her eyes. And although she could not quite grasp them, a sense of warmth and delight stayed with her when her eyes opened once more.

Glancing around the dark room, Christine swallowed as she remembered the feel of Wesley's hands on her body and the touch of his lips on her own. In her dream, he had whispered, 'Marry me,' only this time, she had said yes.

With trembling hands, Christine shot upright and wrapped her arms around her knees as she cursed for all she was worth. How dare that…that…man infiltrate her dreams? Was she insane? Thinking of accepting his proposal? No, no, no. She hadn't thought it. She had merely dreamt it, and dreams, they were just insignificant musings, were they not?

Greatly disturbed by her own willingness to forget about her principles and marry Wesley no matter how fatal that would eventually prove to be, Christine fled from her bed. With limbs that simply could not be persuaded to calm, she paced her room once again, afraid that her dreams were a bad omen, precursors of what was to come if she gave in to the tender emotions that had so unexpectedly taken root in her heart. What had he done to her?

Afraid of what *she* might do, of what *she* might agree to the next time she laid eyes on him, Christine threw on a riding habit and carefully cracked open the door. When the coast remained clear and the house continued to slumber peacefully, she tiptoed out into the hallway and then down the stairs. Although the tiny hairs on the back of her neck stood on end, no one stopped her. Pulling a cloak around her against the cold, she slipped outside and headed for the stables.

As her teeth began to chatter, Christine pushed onward, her head slightly bent to escape the stinging wind that brushed over her face and pulled on her hair. At least, it was not snowing anymore.

When she finally slipped into the stables, she didn't even mind the somewhat reeking warmth that engulfed her. Tiptoeing along the row of horseboxes, Christine stopped when a soft nicker reached her ear. A smile on her face, she turned to the silver-grey mare curiously stretching her nose toward her.

Then she stopped. What was she doing? Sneaking out of the house in the middle of the night to go…where exactly?

Closing her eyes, Christine took a deep breath. It was highly unusual for her not to have a plan, not to know what came next. However, in that moment, she couldn't even think of making a plan. All she could think of was to get away!

With her mind made up and no alternative presenting itself, Christine quickly led the mare from the box before she craned her neck, trying to locate a suitable bridle and saddle.

"Who's there?"

Startled, Christine spun around just as an old man, a stable hand from the looks of it, came limping toward her. Swallowing, she straightened her shoulders.

"Who are you?" he demanded as his eyes slid over her.

"I'm a guest here," Christine stated, disdain dripping from her voice. What else was she supposed to say? After all, it was true, was it not? "And you are?"

At her words, his eyes widened slightly, and a hint of recognition came to them. "The name's Milton," he said, his own voice laced with disrespect, and despite the dim light, Christine could see only too well what he thought of her. "Is there anything I can help you with,…Miss?" He might as well have said *mistress*. Apparently, it hadn't taken long for gossip to spread!

Trying to remain unaffected by his rudeness, Christine raised her chin a fraction. "Saddle my horse." Normally, she would have asked, but right then and there, she wasn't in the mood. It took all the willpower she had to fight down the urge to defend herself and set things right. Conjuring her sister's face, Christine stilled her trembling hands and bit back the snide comments that would have saved her dignity.

"Yes, Miss."

When she finally left Sanford Manor behind, the imprints of her mare's hooves in the soft snow all that remained, Christine breathed a sigh of relief. Although she did not know where she was headed, it felt heavenly to have escaped her prison cell as well as the temptations that threatened.

The early morning air, crisp and fresh in her lungs, chased away the night's dreams, and she turned toward the horizon where touches of dark red and purple began to dance across the sky. Christine sighed at the beautiful sight before her when she realised that returning before dawn was now out of the question.

Too occupied with her internal battles, she hadn't noticed how late—or rather early—it was. Ought she turn back? After all, all she wanted or rather needed—desperately so—were a few moments of peace. A few moments to collect her thoughts lest she lose her wits within earshot of the servants. Last night had proved beyond the shadow of a doubt that Wesley Everett knew well how to unsettle her. In the face of his proposal, she found herself unable to remain rational.

Again, a shiver ran down her back, and for a moment, Christine closed her eyes, remembering the soft touch of his lips.

No! Her mind screamed. She couldn't return. Not now. Not yet. At least not until she had reclaimed her faculties.

Again, her sister's image drifted before her inner eye, and Christine swallowed. "I shall only be gone a moment," she whispered into the morning air. "I promise I shall not ruin our plan."

Riding onward, Christine remembered Wesley telling her of a nearby neighbor, and for a moment, she hesitated, glancing in all directions, trying to determine what direction to avoid. Although she longed for human companionship—however, not that of Wesley Everett—Christine knew well that it would be foolish to seek out Sanford Manor's only neighbour. After all, there was no way for her to explain…

As she could not recall where Stanhope Grove—if that was even the correct name—was located, Christine decided to follow the sunrise and spurred on her mare before she could lose her nerve.

What had this man done to her? Never had she been hesitant in her decisions. Never had she doubted her own wits. Never had she run away.

Never!

For a second, Christine was about to turn around and face Wesley, no matter the consequences. However, once more, an image of her sister's tear-streaked face stopped her.

Shaking her head, Christine urged her mare on toward the sunrise. She could not risk her sister's happiness. At least for now, she needed to put a little distance between herself and Wesley Everett, and then she would return…and face him.

Turning down a small slope, Christine enjoyed the horse's movements as they flew across the snow-covered world. She could only hope that she would not accidentally stumble upon Stanhope Grove.

However, even if she did, she could simply turn back. After all, who would be foolish enough to be riding out in this weather at the break of dawn?

The night had been one long torment. Unable to forget or even temporarily ignore Christine's *threat*, Wesley found himself picturing his worst nightmare again and again: the woman he…Christine in another man's arms.

Something had to be done!

Dressing in haste before the sun had even fully risen, Wesley stalked down into the kitchen and ordered an opulent breakfast to be served in the upstairs parlour. Although he was still intent on keeping her true identity a secret, Wesley knew that confining her to her room for much longer would prove fatal. Of that he was certain.

Raking his mind, Wesley tried to think of ways he could keep her entertained and in a good mood without agreeing to her scandalous, though tempting proposal. He wanted her to be happy, and maybe, just maybe, it would aid him in changing her mind. Maybe if he proved to her that they would always enjoy each other's company, she would be willing to reconsider her answer.

As his eyes swept across the downstairs parlour, he called for Thompson.

"Yes, sir." Like a ghost hovering in the corner of the room, he suddenly materialised behind Wesley, who spun around startled.

"Ah, there you are." Gesturing toward the old wooden chess board that had been in his father's family for generations, Wesley said, "Please, have this moved upstairs into…our guest's bedchamber as soon as she wakes."

A hint of disapproval in his eyes, his butler cleared his throat. "As far as I know the…lady has already risen," he said in a tone as though speaking the words made him physically ill. "I was informed that she took a horse from the stables early this morning."

Staring at Thompson, Wesley swallowed. "She did what? Where did she go?" Fear gripped his heart as he forced himself to remain calm. Where could she have gone in this weather?

"I'm afraid I'm not privileged to that information, sir."

Gritting his teeth, Wesley took a deep breath to keep himself from strangling the old man. No matter who Thompson thought she was, did it not concern him that a young woman unfamiliar with the terrain had ridden out in this weather all alone?

The more Wesley thought about it, the more his head began to spin. "Have my horse saddled immediately!" he hissed at Thompson. "And bring me my coat." Then he rushed upstairs to slip into his tall winter boots.

If anything happened to Christine...

Shaking his head, he tried to concentrate on the task at hand. It would do Christine no good if he merely worried about her. He had to find her! But how?

Swinging himself into the saddle of the chestnut bay gelding, Wesley let his eyes sweep over the landscape before him. Apart from Sanford Manor, meadows and the beginnings of a forest was all he could see as it lay covered by a thick layer of snow. Urging his mount down the drive, he leaned forward as something caught his eye.

There in the snow were hoof prints leading eastward!

As his heart danced with relief, Wesley spurred on his gelding, his eyes fixed on the delicate trail Christine had left. He felt as though he were following breadcrumbs she had left for him to find. Thank goodness it hadn't snowed the night before!

With excitement coursing through his veins, Wesley barely felt the sting of cold air on his face as he flew across the meadow, nearing the forest. Here and there, he would slow down because the tracks turned in one direction before circling back and then heading into the other. Where was she going? Did she even have a destination in mind or was she simply roaming the countryside? The latter was the one more likely, after all, she had never even been to Sanford Manor before and, therefore, did not know her way around.

Had Catherine ever mentioned anything to her? Maybe before they'd left. No, Wesley shook his head as he continued to follow her trail. Why would she have? The only one who had ever...

Wesley froze, then slapped his gloved hand to his forehead in annoyance.

The only one who had ever spoken to her about Sanford Manor and surroundings had been him.

Wesley cringed at the memory of their carriage ride when he had in all innocence mentioned that Lord Stanhope's estate was located about a two-hour ride eastward. Although he had merely done so to assure her that no one would accidentally stumble upon them—after all, no one in their right mind would brace the outdoors in such weather to visit one's neighbours—it now appeared to have been quite unwise, for Christine could, for all intents and purposes, not be considered in her right mind, could she?

Cursing under his breath, Wesley urged his gelding onward. No wonder she was not travelling in a direct line. She only had a vague idea of where the estate was located.

For a moment, Wesley debated with himself whether to follow her tracks or take the shortest route to Stanhope Grove. Although a part of him worried that she had simply ridden by the estate without coming upon it, Wesley decided on the more direct approach. After all, Christine was an intelligent, resourceful woman, and he had no doubt that she would find her way. If she was determined to find Stanhope Grove, she would!

Spurring on his gelding, Wesley hurried onward, and before long, Stanhope Grove came into view. Encircled by dense growing groves on three sides, it lay snug in a small valley, a stream running alongside it, giving water to the large granite well decorating the front gardens.

With eyes searching his surroundings—as though expecting Christine to jump out at him from behind one of the well-manicured, snow-covered bushes by the front entrance—Wesley handed his gelding's reins to a stable hand and then proceeded up the front stairs.

The door swung open as he approached, and Stanhope's butler bowed low. "Good day, sir."

"Good day," Wesley mumbled, still on the lookout. "Is Lord Stanhope in?"

"He is, sir. Allow me to lead the way."

Proceeding through the large front hall, their footsteps echoing in the high-vaulted room, Wesley followed Stanhope's butler to the front drawing room. As they approached, voices echoed to his ears, and one in particular nearly stopped his heart.

"How marvellous!" Christine exclaimed, her voice ringing with joy and exuberance that had been absent in the past few days. "A Christmas Ball is a truly wonderful idea!"

"Is it not?" Eleanor Abbott, Stanhope's younger sister, beamed. "And the masks make it even more spectacular!"

"They do indeed."

Stepping into the drawing room, Wesley found all eyes turn to him.

Whereas Christine's eyes widened ever so slightly betraying her surprise to see him there, Stanhope as well as his mother regarded him with drawn brows clearly showing their disapproval. What on earth had Christine told them? He could only hope that she had not revealed herself as his mistress. He shook off that thought. Even Christine had better sense than to ruin herself so willingly, did she not?

"Wesley," his friend greeted him coldly, his face almost immobile. "How kind of you to pay us a visit." Through narrowed eyes, he regarded Wesley, then almost imperceptibly shook his head as though chiding him for cheating in a card game.

"It's such a beautiful morning," Wesley said, forcing a polite smile on his face, "that I thought a quick ride would be quite enjoyable."

"I see," Stanhope mumbled. Then he bowed to the ladies. "Excuse us." Striding toward the door, his eyes ordered Wesley to follow him.

Out in the hall, Stanhope walked a few quick paces down the corridor before he turned to face his friend. "Are you out of your mind?" he asked, his voice betraying a slight tremble as he sought to control his obvious outrage.

"Arthur, I can expl—"

"Explain?" Shaking his head, Stanhope began to pace up and down the corridor. "What on earth possessed you? I've known you to do a great many...*questionable* things in your time, but this!" He pointed back at the closed door to the drawing room. "Do you truly have no scruples?"

Gritting his teeth, Wesley feared the worst. "What did she tell you?"

Stanhope snorted. "That she is a guest in your house, and that you were separated when riding out this morning."

Hearing his friend's answer, Wesley relaxed before a frown drew down his brows. "Then why do you look so distraught?"

Hands on his hips, Stanhope glared at him. "What she didn't say has me more concerned. The moment I came upon her out in the woods—and let me assure you I was quite taken aback to find an unchaperoned woman riding across my land—the look on her face told me more than I cared to know."

For as long as they had known each other, Wesley had never been able to understand his friend beyond formal niceties. For all intents and purposes, it seemed as though Arthur Abbott, Earl of Stanhope, had never experienced a desire of his own. All he knew—and was fond of—were society's rules, of which he never failed to remind his fellow men. Truly, Christine could not have sought refuge with a more inconvenient person. What had he been thinking taking her to Sanford Manor?

"What do you mean?" Wesley asked, forcing himself not to drop his gaze. If Stanhope found out who Christine truly was—what name had she given him?—would he feel compelled to reveal her identity?

"Do not take me for a fool, Wesley," Stanhope snapped, taking a step closer, his hawk-like eyes drilling into Wesley's soul. "Although I do not know who she truly is—Christine Smith seems rather unlikely—I have no doubt that she is a proper young lady, which makes me wonder what she is doing in your company," Stanhope hissed, "and without a chaperone no less."

Wesley sighed. "It's complicated."

"I doubt that very much," his friend snapped, once more shaking his head. "You know as well as I do that the code of conduct must be upheld at all times. Therefore, I must question your intentions."

A short chuckle escaped Wesley. *His* intentions? Had *he* not been the one to ask her to marry him? And had *she* not been the one to refuse?

However, as his friend was unaware of their history, he mistook Wesley's reaction for a lack of morals. "This is serious," Stanhope warned. "Your thoughtless behaviour could cost her her reputation, and as you are well aware of, a reputation once lost is gone forever. Do you truly wish that fate upon her?"

"Not at all," Wesley assured his friend, hoping that his voice sounded as sincere as his hopes were for a future with Christine. "I beg you to believe me that my intentions are truly honourable." He sighed. "I cannot explain at the moment, however, it is at the utmost importance that she and I return to Sanford Manor at once."

Stanhope's eyes widened. "You expect me to allow her to return with you? Again, without a chaperone?" He shook his head. "I could not do so in good conscience."

Wesley's hopes sank. "Then what do you propose?"

"As long as you refuse to provide me with her actual identity," Stanhope said, annoyance in his voice, "so that I may call upon her relatives to retrieve her, I'm afraid I must insist on her staying at Stanhope Grove. Here, at least, my mother's as well as my sister's presence shall assure that no harm come to her reputation."

Closing his eyes, Wesley sighed. This was worse than expected, and yet, he probably shouldn't be surprised at all for Arthur Abbott, Earl of Stanhope, had never met a rule he didn't like or felt compelled to obey.

FOR A LADY'S REPUTATION

"Of you'll promise to stay for luncheon," Eleanor beamed, almost tripping over her words in her eagerness to gain Christine's acceptance, "I shall show you the mask I had fashioned for the ball. It is quite splendid, I assure you."

"I'm certain it is." Awfully tempted to stay at Stanhope Grove for as long as possible, Christine glanced at the door through which Wesley and Lord Stanhope had left. Now, that her *warden* had found her—not that she could blame him for it certainly had been her doing—she had very little hope of an extended stay, and so she did not dare accept Eleanor's kind invitation. "I most certainly would love to stay on," she admitted, "however, I am unaware of Mr. Everett's current plans and can, therefore, not accept without conferring with him first."

"I understand," Eleanor said, her spirits a little subdued but still hopeful. "Then we shall ask him as soon as he returns."

Glancing at Lady Stanhope, Christine thought to detect more than just a hint of disapproval in the older lady's watchful grey eyes. They seemed like those of a bird of prey, clear and sharp, able to detect every movement in their surroundings, and currently, they were trained on Christine.

From the slight crinkle of Lady Stanhope's nose as well as the way she had raised her chin when looking at her, Christine was fairly certain that Lord Stanhope's mother did not approve of her. Was it just a general dislike? Christine wondered. Or did she suspect something untoward? Remembering the manner in which she had shown up on their doorstep as well as her made-up explanation for her presence, Christine could not fault her for thinking the worst.

Sighing, she felt like hanging her head. It wasn't even noon yet, and already at least two people had looked at her with disregard, thinking her a man's mistress!

Christine knew it bothered her more than she liked to admit especially since she could not defend herself. After all, whenever people would accuse another of something, it was rarely done to their face but rather whispered about behind their back.

And yet, despite the uncomfortable feelings Lady Stanhope's disdainful looks stirred within her, Christine's heart wilted at the thought of returning to Sanford Manor and being *locked* away in that sad, little room. She'd much rather spent the remainder of the day at Stanhope Grove, conversing with young Eleanor. Especially after Wesley had made it perfectly clear that he had no intention of…accepting her proposal.

"Eleanor," Lady Stanhope said, rising from the settee, "I believe you have not yet finished the embroidery on…that cushion." Glancing at Christine, she stepped toward the door, her eyes narrowing. "I suggest you take your leave."

"But, Mother," Eleanor began before her shoulders slumped and she turned to Christine, an apologetic and openly regretful look in her pale blue eyes. "It's been such a pleasure to make your acquaintance, and I truly hope that Mr. Everett's schedule allows you to extend your visit."

"As do I," Christine replied whole-heartedly.

Ushering her daughter out of the room, Lady Stanhope fixed Christine with a last, hard look before she almost imperceptibly shook her head in open disapproval that left no doubt in Christine's mind just how low her opinion was of her.

Finding herself alone in a room once again, Christine sighed. This was truly an unfortunate Christmas season; as uneventful as any she had ever experienced. She could only hope that her thoughtless behaviour hadn't ruined it for her sister as well. Oh, if only Lord Stanhope hadn't been out that early! What had the man been thinking? Come to think of it, all this was actually his fault for...for...

Christine cursed under her breath, knowing only too well that there was no way she would be able to convince even herself that none of this had been her doing. If only Wesley hadn't proposed! If only she hadn't found herself tempted!

Closing her eyes for a moment, an image of her sister's tear-streaked face appeared before Christine's inner eye, and a pang of guilt ricocheted through her. She truly ought to be more grateful for the trifles that bothered her in life compared to the desperate fear that threatened to consume Catherine. If only she knew how things were going at Harrington Park!

However, Christine had little time to dwell on such musings for only a moment after Lady Stanhope and Eleanor had left, the door opened once more and Wesley as well as Lord Stanhope stepped inside. While the young lord stayed back, taking up position in the corner by the door, his eyes averted, and yet, glancing in their direction, Wesley walked over to her, his face pale and his shoulders tense.

Rising from the armchair she had occupied for the past hour, Christine stepped toward him, a lump in her throat as she met his eyes. "Is something wrong?" she whispered, eyes shifting to Lord Stanhope.

Wesley sighed. "It most certainly is."

A cold shiver ran down Christine's back as she saw the hint of torment in his eyes. "What happened? Why is he here?"

Wesley chuckled. "He is here to assure that no harm comes to your precious reputation."

For a moment, Christine merely stared at him. "What? What did you tell him?"

"What did *I* tell him?" Wesley snapped, fighting to keep his voice down. "What were *you* thinking leaving as you did? Do you have any idea how much trouble we're in right now?"

Christine sighed. "I'm sorry, but I just...I had to get out of the house. I never meant to come here. I assure you, and I hope that you can believe me." Remembering her dream, she took a step backward, suddenly all too aware of his presence. "I needed a little bit of distance."

Gritting his teeth, Wesley took a slow breath. "Whatever the reason, coming here changed everything."

"What do you mean? Are we not returning to Sanford Manor?" Once more, Christine glanced at Lord Stanhope. His eyes shone in a clear grey, just like his mother's. However, while his mother's had been cold and calculating, the young lord's held concern and compassion.

"Unfortunately, not." Shifting his eyes to his friend for but a moment, Wesley sighed. "The situation is as follows: my dear friend, Lord Stanhope, is a very enthusiastic advocate for maintaining proper etiquette at all times. Therefore, he refuses to allow us to leave together—unchaperoned as we are—because he fears for your reputation. Despite your refusal to give your real name—"

Christine's eyes widened.

"Yes, you're not as good a liar as you thought you were," Wesley chided. "Well, as I was about to say: despite your refusal to give your real name, he is convinced that you are not...let's say, without morals, but a proper lady. Therefore, he is determined to protect your reputation at all cost." A devilish grin came to his face. "Looks like you found another knight in shining armour ready to protect your honour." He shook his head. "If he only knew how little it means to you." A hint of pain rang in his voice, and Christine felt his hurtful remark like a stab to the heart. Simply because she had...Did that mean she had no honour? Apparently, not as far as society was concerned.

Today was truly a day she wished she could forget.

"What does that mean?" Christine asked, determined not to allow his words to dampen her spirit. "Am I to stay here?"

Wesley nodded, a touch of sadness in his eyes.

Christine took a slow breath as she realised the implications of his words. Oh, how thoughtless she had been! Although she could not have anticipated precisely this outcome, she admitted—at least to herself—that she ought to have done as he had asked and stayed at Sanford Manor. Then, at least, she would not have been parted from...

Again, she took a deep breath as sorrow filled her heart. Despite their continued arguing and her earlier desire to avoid him, Christine could not imagine spending the next few days or even weeks without him.

After all, Wesley was...he was...

"As his mother and sister are in residence," Wesley continued, "he believes that you are safest here."

"I see," Christine mumbled as she gazed up into his eyes; eyes that looked into hers in a way that made her feel safer than she ever had while at the same time had her catch her breath as her body itched to feel his arms come around her and his lips cover hers.

"Thankfully," Wesley continued, the ghost of a smirk on his face as he held her gaze, "considering that the need for a chaperone is met, he granted my request to stay in one of the guest rooms."

Christine drew in a deep breath as relief flooded her, and for a moment, she closed her eyes. Then a deep smile spread over her face, and looking up at him, she delighted in the mischievous twinkle that suddenly lit up his eyes. What had happened? He had seemed so disappointed in her only a moment ago, had he not?

"I hope you do not mind my presence here," Wesley teased, the sparkle in his eyes telling her that he knew she did not.

Christine smiled. "I never minded your presence, only your proposal."

8

LADY ELEANOR'S DEMAND

*T*heir first day at Stanhope Grove passed in quiet comfort or rather discomfort as far as Lady Stanhope was concerned.

After Eleanor had dragged Christine upstairs in order to show her some kind of accessory—as far as Wesley could remember—Wesley had found himself on his way to his friend's study when the door had suddenly opened and Lady Stanhope had rushed out, her face a twisted snarl.

Upon seeing him, she had stopped in her tracks.

With a polite smile on his face, Wesley had bowed to her, deciding it would be far easier on all of them not to antagonise the lady of the house.

However, all his attempts had been in vain as the lady in question had glared at him through narrowed eyes, her nose twitching with disgust, before she had strode past him, barely glancing at him with her head held high as though he were a lowly servant.

Wesley guessed that Lady Stanhope doubted Christine's story as much as her son. However, while the son had made assumptions—correct assumptions, Wesley had to admit—in favour of Christine, his mother had done the opposite.

Wesley could only hope she would refrain from spreading any rumours for fear of staining her own family's reputation should it become known that their hospitality had at one point extended to *such* a woman.

For the millionth time, Wesley cursed Christine for her ludicrous idea! Or ideas as it were for she appeared to stumble from one to the next as easily as other people changed the topic of their conversation.

"Do not worry," his friend spoke out behind him as Wesley was still staring after Lady Stanhope, wondering if there even *was* a way to fix all that had happened in the past few hours. "She will not say a word even if only for Eleanor's sake as well as my own."

Turning to his friend, Wesley sighed, "I hope you're right."

"Will you not tell me what's going on?" Lord Stanhope asked, stepping aside to allow Wesley to pass. Then he closed the door behind them and took the seat behind his desk across from his friend. "I give you my word, I will not speak of this to anyone."

Again, Wesley sighed. If there was anyone in the world whose word was beyond the shadow of a doubt, it was Stanhope's. "To tell you the truth," he began, rubbing his temples, "it's fairly complicated. Every once in a while, I feel as though even *I* do not understand what's going on."

Stanhope snorted. "I've never seen you relinquish control to anyone." Then the amusement left his face, and for a long moment, he regarded his friend with open curiosity. "You care about her, do you not?"

Cringing slightly, Wesley met his friend's eyes. "I'm afraid so."

Stanhope laughed. "Do you consider it unfortunate to be in love?"

Wesley took a deep breath. Was he in love? He shook his head. He would dwell on that question later. "Not generally so. However, Christine is…" Again, he shook his head, at a loss for words.

"Then her name truly is Christine?" his friend asked, his hawk-like eyes watching Wesley's every move.

Wesley nodded.

"And her family name?"

Wesley swallowed. "Dansby."

Stanhope's mouth dropped open before a spark of understanding came to his grey eyes. "Catherine's sister." He shook his head. "I knew she looked familiar. I cannot believe I did not see it right away." Leaning back in his chair, he regarded Wesley, his brows slowly drawing down in confusion. "However, I must admit that knowing her true identity, I feel as though I am even farther from understanding what's going on."

Shrugging his shoulders, Wesley snorted. "It all began with another one of Christine's ludicrous ideas," he started as his friend rested his head against the back of his chair, listening intently.

"It is exquisite!" Christine exclaimed, delightedly turning the mask in her hands. The golden ornaments sparkled in the sun shining in through the window, giving it a magical glow. "And it matches your dress perfectly."

"Does it not?" Eleanor asked, gazing almost lovingly at her lavender ball gown reserved for the Christmas Ball. "I've never owned anything so beautiful."

Setting down the mask, Christine stepped closer, her eyes gliding over Eleanor's glowing face. Eyes distant, the young woman barely seemed to see the dress. Her gaze appeared directed inward as she pictured something…or rather someone beloved, and a deep smile came to her face.

Brushing a hand down Eleanor's arm, Christine said, "Who is he?"

As though startled awake, the young woman flinched, her eyes restless as she brushed past Christine and strode toward the window. "Who do you speak of?" she asked, her voice, however, hitched slightly, and a crimson red came to her cheeks.

"The young man who seems to be occupying your thoughts," Christine said, coming to stand next to Eleanor. "Will he be at the Christmas Ball?"

Eleanor swallowed, then slowly turned her gaze to Christine, the corners of her mouth straining upward as she fought the smile that threatened to light up her face. "I must not speak of him," she whispered, then clamped a hand over her mouth as though she had already said too much.

Christine laughed. "I dare say you do appear quite taken with this young man…whoever he is. Will you not give me his name?" she asked, and a teasing tone came to her voice as she went on. "Or are you afraid that speaking his name will conjure him here?"

Eleanor's face turned white as a sheet, and she shook her head vehemently.

"What's the matter?" Christine asked, all amusement gone from her voice. A blind man could see that Eleanor had lost her heart to the young man she didn't dare speak of. But why didn't she dare? What on earth could be the matter? "Is he not a suitable match?" Christine asked when Eleanor remained silent.

A large tear formed in the young woman's left eye, then spilled over and slowly ran down her cheek as she tried to blink it away. "Mother does not approve of him," she cried, trying her best to suppress the heart-wrenching sobs that escaped her throat.

"Oh, dear," Christine mumbled, pulling the young woman into her arms.

Doing her best to calm her, Christine pictured Lady Stanhope's glaring eyes and determinedly set chin as she had regarded their unexpected visitor—namely her—with disapproval. Indeed, with a mother like that, there was very little hope for a happily-ever-after for Eleanor. If Lady Stanhope was dead set against the man who had captured her daughter's heart, no one on this earth could change her mind.

Christine's heart wept for the young woman. "Your mother is not here," she whispered. "Tell me about him." If nothing else, she could let Eleanor speak her mind and listen to the troubles of her heart. Unfortunately, all Christine had to offer was her sympathy.

Sniffling, Eleanor sank onto the settee. "His name is Henry Waltham," she whispered, her eyes darting to the door as though her mother would barge in any second.

"Henry Waltham?" Christine asked, taking the seat next to Eleanor. "He's not one of Lord Caulfield's sons, is he?"

Dabbing a handkerchief to her eyes, Eleanor nodded. "The youngest," she sobbed, "which is one of the reasons Mother disapproves."

Trying to remember what she knew of Lord Caulfield's sons, Christine frowned as nothing good came to mind. In fact, her path had occasionally crossed those of Stephen and Andrew Waltham, and as far as she could remember they were wastrels, drinking and gambling and spending their father's money wherever they could.

Considering that Lord Caulfield and his baroness had always been well-thought of members of society, their sons had always seemed a harsher than deserved punishment for some unknown faux pas. In recent years, society at large had speculated about the potential skeletons in the baron's cupboard.

Shaking her head, Eleanor looked almost pleadingly at Christine, who wished with all her heart that there was something she could do to help. "Mother was quite put out when I did not procure a husband during my first season," Eleanor admitted, a touch of embarrassment in her eyes. "I tried to find someone I could see myself marrying, believe me, but no one even compared to Henry." Her hands began to tremble, and new tears formed in her eyes. "And now, she insists that I choose a *suitable* husband next season. She's made it perfectly clear that anything less is not an option."

Christine sighed, grateful for her own parents' generosity in considering their daughters' heart's desire. "Have you spoken to your brother?" she asked, remembering the kindness in those grey eyes.

Eleanor shook her head. "Mother would be furious if she knew I was trying to go against her wishes. I barely managed to voice my objections to her. She is…she is…"

Christine nodded. "I know."

"The Christmas Ball is all I have left," Eleanor whispered, eyes once more shifting to the door. "If I am to choose a husband next season, then my only wish is to enjoy one night with the man I love." An innocent sparkle came to her eyes. "I want to dance and laugh and…" Biting her lower lip, she stopped, a rosy glow coming to her cheeks.

"And?" Christine pressed.

Eleanor swallowed, then straightened her shoulders and met Christine's eyes with an unwavering gaze. "And I want a kiss under the mistletoe," she stated. "In fact, I demand one. So that I will always remember what it feels like to be kissed by a man I love."

9

TO LOVE OR NOT TO LOVE

*T*he following week, Christine found herself unusually reflective. Whenever she did not sit with Eleanor, doing her best to lift the young woman's spirits, or exchange a careful word with Wesley under the watchful eyes of their host, Christine wandered from room to room, gazing out the windows, lost in thought.

Eleanor's confession had stirred something deep within her, and Christine began to wonder if she was making a mistake. The doomed love that lived in the young woman's heart and frequently spilled down her cheeks made Christine cherish the freedom she herself had. The freedom to choose. And yet, long ago, she had made the *choice* to remain unmarried, free of the burdens marriage would inevitably bring.

But was it truly inevitable?

"Are you betrothed?" Eleanor asked her one snowy afternoon as they sat alone in the drawing room. While the younger woman tended to her embroidery, Christine once again found herself standing by the window, staring out at the white blanket draped over the earth.

"Betrothed?" The question jolted her awake, and she turned to look at Eleanor. "Why do you ask?"

"Well, I admit I'm curious," Eleanor said, eyes darting back and forth between Christine as well as the cushion and needle in her hands. "You're so delightful. Men must be fighting for your hand in marriage, and yet, you're still unmarried after all the seasons you must have—" Eyes going wide, Eleanor dropped the cushion and needle and clamped a hand over her mouth.

Watching her with amusement, Christine chuckled.

"I'm sorry," Eleanor whispered, an embarrassed glow coming to her cheeks. "I did not mean to say that you're…"

"Old?" Christine asked, then she shook her head and laughed. "Do not worry, dear Eleanor. I'm well aware that I'm not a young girl anymore."

After taking a couple of deep breaths, Eleanor seemed to relax. "I was just curious," she whispered once again, her eyes returning to her embroidery.

"No," Christine answered, taking a seat next to her. "I'm not betrothed, and I don't ever intend to be."

Again, Eleanor's eyes bulged. "Why ever not?"

Christine shrugged. "That is difficult to explain. I…"

"But I thought you were betrothed to Wesley Everett," Eleanor interrupted, her cushion all but forgotten. "Whenever you enter a room, he immediately notices. He always takes a deep breath as though he feels the need to steady his nerves in your presence and his eyes follow you everywhere." A deep smile came to her lips. "He looks at you the same way…," her voice dropped to a whisper, "the same way Henry looks at me."

Christine swallowed as she couldn't help but notice that her heart jumped with joy. Did he truly care for her? Did he love her? Had Wesley not always been the kind of man who knew how to enjoy life and would only take a wife because it was expected of him, not because he wanted to?

However, what was even more confusing was that her heart seemed to be enjoying Eleanor's observation, sending a myriad of butterflies into her belly. Christine couldn't help but wonder whether her reaction to him was merely due to his physical attraction or whether it spoke of a much deeper bond. Her mind, though, didn't dare consider that option.

"I admit I do care for him," Christine said, knowing that denying the obvious would only increase Eleanor's curiosity. "However, I do not believe in marriage."

As expected, the young woman's eyes opened wide. "You don't...? What do you mean? The only reason a woman does not get married is because she cannot procure a husband. Why would you choose not to marry?"

Christine sighed, doubting the wisdom of sharing her innermost thoughts on the constitution of marriage with a young woman in love like Eleanor. "Because love doesn't always last," she finally said, hoping her words would not offend her companion. "I've found myself...let's say, taken with a man before. However, eventually my feelings have always disappeared. What if I had married one of these men? Then I would be trapped in a loveless marriage and might even find myself longing for another man." Shaking her head, Christine looked at Eleanor's eager face. "I'm not the kind of woman to betray a promise once given. I'd rather not promise anything I am not certain I can keep."

Eleanor nodded. "I admit your words have merit," she said, suddenly sounding older than her years, "and I understand the worry that lives in your heart. However, maybe you've never truly been in love." An apologetic smile on her face, she met Christine's eyes. "I do not mean to offend you, but maybe you've never been tempted to marry because you've never been in love."

Christine took a deep breath.

"Love is," sighing, Eleanor gazed into the distance, a deep smile on her young face, "it is all-consuming and powerful. Although, yes, I admit sometimes it does not last a lifetime, it is well-worth the risk. Even if it fades eventually, in exchange for its loss, you've had years of unbelievable bliss."

A soft smile came to Christine's face as she watched her young friend.

"However, as intense as an infatuation might be," Eleanor continued, "it rarely survives the daily struggles it often faces and quickly burns out. It is no match for love."

A smile on her face, Christine shook her head and gently placed her hand on Eleanor's. "You're wise for someone so young," she said, admiration ringing in her voice.

A soft blush came to Eleanor's cheeks. "I've thought about this a lot," she admitted. "I know that if I do not marry Henry but another, my life will be a life of regret. However, I find myself unable to go against everything I was raised to be." She dropped her gaze, her fingers twirling the needle's thread. "Henry has never asked," she admitted quietly. "In moments of doubt, I feel uncertain if it is because he knows we have no future or if it is because he does not love me as much as I love him."

Christine sighed. Since she had never seen them together, she could not offer any reassurance on the matter. However, would it even be wise to do so? After all, Eleanor knew as well as she did herself that there was little to no chance for a happily-ever-after for the two of them. Ought she feed the young woman's hopes when they would likely be crushed before the end of the next season?

Once again, Christine realised how fortunate she was not to be pressured into accepting a man she did not care for merely because he was suitable in the eyes of her parents. She had the choice to choose a man she loved, and yet, she spurned her fortune at every turn.

For once, Christine did not wonder whether Wesley loved her or whether she loved him, but instead she thought about whether or not—if that were the case—she ought to marry for love? Or was Eleanor's emphatic speech messing with her rationally achieved principles? And who ought to decide? Her heart or her mind?

While Christine spent most of her time in Eleanor's company, Wesley found himself wandering the halls of Stanhope Grove alone. Although his friend often sought him out, asking questions that Wesley didn't dare answer, Wesley's monosyllabic answers would quickly drive him from his side.

"I've never known you to be this glum," Lord Stanhope observed, his sharp eyes watching him. "I fail to understand why you do not simply ask for her hand in marriage. You're quite obviously taken with her."

Not meeting his friend's eyes, Wesley cleared his throat. "It is not that simple."

"In the past week, you've said so a thousand times," Lord Stanhope observed, "and yet, I fail to see the complication you're referring to."

Wesley shook his head. What was he to say? Never had he thought of himself as one to fall head over heels in love with a woman he hardly knew, and when it finally had happened, he had done his best to ignore her, banish her from his thoughts and more importantly from his heart. But what good had it done him?

The second their paths had crossed once more, he had lost his heart to her all over again.

And as though fortune had a cruel sense of irony, she had refused him. However, he couldn't very well confess such a thing to Stanhope, could he?

"Does her heart belong to another?" his friend asked when Wesley remained quiet, still contemplating how best to evade these continued questions.

Dear God, I hope not!

Gritting his teeth, Wesley forced air into his lungs, willing his heart to slow to a more moderate pace. "Not as far as I know," he finally admitted, hoping that what he said was true. After all, she had never spoken of love. She had only ever…invited him into her bed. Did she even care for him? Or was he simply an opportunity to test her newest theory?

As Wesley continued to stare out the window, his friend shook his head, then placed a comforting hand on his shoulder. "I may not be the most reliable judge in these matters," he said, "but I do believe that she cares for you." Then he stepped back and walked away.

Squaring his shoulders, Wesley felt his hands begin to tremble as his heart danced in his chest, and he had to fight the glowing smile that lifted the corners of his mouth. Stanhope was a man of principle and truthfulness. Not unlike Wesley himself, he knew very little about matters of the heart and had in all likelihood misinterpreted Christine's behaviour. After all, considering the frank and open way she had always spoken to him, she had not once said anything about love.

Did you? A little voice whispered, but Wesley instantly shushed it.

"Oh!"

That soft, slightly breathless exclamation jolted Wesley from his thoughts, and he spun around to find the woman he…Christine standing just inside the door. One hand on the handle, she seemed to hesitate as her eyes searched his face, a hint of a rosy blush colouring her cheeks.

It only took Wesley one moment to realise that something was different.

Gone was the self-assured and daring woman, who had never flinched under anyone's gaze, who had never dropped her eyes in embarrassment or refrained from speaking whatever was on her mind.

The woman who now stood across from him seemed a mere shadow of the lady who had stolen his heart. Her eyes barely met his, and she gnawed on her lower lip, a nervous tremble in her hands. "I should leave," she whispered as though she were a debutante afraid of the repercussions of being discovered in a man's presence without a chaperone.

Wesley snorted at the thought, and her head snapped up, her eyes meeting his. "Do you suddenly fear for your reputation?" he asked, strolling toward her, his gaze trained on her face, curiously watching her reaction.

A familiar smile lit up her face, and a hint of mischief came to her eyes as she firmly closed the door behind her. "Not at all," Christine said, her gaze resting on his as he moved toward her. "I merely thought to spare our hostess the shock should she happen to come upon us. The poor lady is quite distraught with our presence in her home."

"How very considerate of you," Wesley mocked as he breathed in the intoxicating scent of her. His head spun, and his hands itched to reach for her as his eyes travelled from hers down to her lips.

A knowing smile curled up her mouth. "But kind sir, I was under the impression that your interest in me was of a purely platonic nature."

Wesley snorted. "What gave you that idea? After all, was it not I who asked for your hand in marriage?"

At his words, Christine sobered and her eyes became serious. "It was, yes," she confirmed, inhaling deeply as she held his gaze. "However, you were also the one who…refused to…" She swallowed before an embarrassed smile came to her face and she bit her lower lip. "You are correct. I do have trouble saying it out loud."

Wesley smiled, delighted with her honesty. "Have you changed your mind?" he asked, stepping closer so that she had to tilt up her head to hold his gaze.

"About *your* proposal?" she asked, a hint of mischief in her eyes. "Or mine?"

Wesley gritted his teeth as his hands settled on her waist. "Mine," he almost growled out, and his arms closed around her possessively.

Trembling, she drew in a sharp breath. Her eyes, however, rested steadily on his. "I have not," she whispered.

His eyes narrowed as his pulse hammered in his veins. "And yours?" he snapped.

Holding his gaze, she shook her head. "I know what I want," she said, a challenge in her tone. "Do you?"

In that moment as he held her in his arms, Wesley couldn't quite recall the reasons for his refusal. He knew exactly what he wanted, and as though of its own volition, his head lowered itself down to hers, his eyes fixed on her lips.

And yet, a quiet voice whispered that that was not all he wanted.

Stopping a hair's breadth from her lips, he looked up into her eyes. "Is it truly of no importance to you whether I care for you or not?" he asked. "Do you not object to a man who only desires your body but does not care the slightest bit for who you are?"

Pressing her lips together, Christine held his gaze, a hint of annoyance in her eyes. "Why do you judge me for something that you've done yourself?"

Swallowing, Wesley stepped back. "I do not judge you."

"You do not?" she mocked, shaking her head. "Then you have exchanged words of love with every woman who has given herself to you?"

"Of course not," Wesley snapped, annoyed with her tendency to generalise their relationship. "That was different. You're—"

"Different?" Christine mocked. "Of course, it is always different for men. A woman has to guard her innocence like a precious good while men boast of the number or their conquests." Shaking her head, she eyed him curiously. "I never thought you were one of those who—"

"I am not," Wesley insisted. His eyes hard, he glared at her, forcing himself to remain calm. How could he make her understand that he did not care the slightest bit what men and women in general did? That he only cared about what *she* did? About what *she* felt?

He took a deep breath. "I don't just want to be *any* man you invite into your bed," he forced out through gritted teeth. "I want...I..."

"What?"

Before he could say another word, a knock sounded on the other side of the door, and they both froze. "Christine, are you in there?" came Eleanor's voice. "A letter was just delivered for you."

10

A WIFE'S RETURN

As the footmen loaded their luggage onto the carriage, Christine stood on the stoop hugging Eleanor. Over the past week, she had grown quite fond of the young woman and desperately wished there was something she could do to help. However, one look at Lady Stanhope's stony face told her that such a wish was futile.

"I wish you could stay," Eleanor cried, brushing away a single tear. "It's been so wonderful," she glanced at her mother, "talking to you."

Christine smiled. "Write to me."

Eleanor nodded vehemently.

"And we shall see each other at the Christmas Ball," Christine reminded her before she hugged Eleanor once more and whispered in her ear. "I shall do what I can to ensure that you receive the kiss you hope for."

Pulling back, Eleanor met her eyes, and a soft smile spread over her face. "Thank you," she whispered. "I've always wondered what it would be like to have a sister to confide in. Now, I know."

With a heavy heart, Christine bid Eleanor goodbye and took her seat in the carriage. A moment later, Wesley joined her, and before long, they were on their way back to Harrington Park.

"What did the letter say?" Wesley asked when Stanhope Grove had disappeared from view.

Turning her head from the window, Christine met his gaze. "She asked us to return."

Wesley sighed. "Yes, you said so," he mumbled, a hint of exasperation in his voice, "but why? Did she not give a reason?"

Christine swallowed, seeing the tension on his face. Holding her gaze, he sat across from her with his body rigid and his muscles clenched, and she had no trouble reading the worry in his blue eyes. "Apparently," she cleared her throat, "William asked for my return."

Wesley's eyes flew open. "He did? What does that mean? Do you think it did not work?"

Christine shrugged as a cold chill crawled down her back. "I have no way of knowing that," she said, her voice almost inaudible. "I can only hope that there is another explanation."

Wesley snorted, a hint of annoyance coming to his face.

Glaring at him, Christine crossed her arms. "Are you saying this is my fault?"

"I didn't say anything!"

"You might as well have," she snapped. "After all, you believed my idea to be ludicrous from the start."

Leaning forward, Wesley met her eyes. "I did, yes, but that doesn't mean I wanted it to fail. He is my brother. I want him to be happy, and I've never seen him as happy as when he was with Catherine."

Dropping her gaze, Christine nodded. "Neither have I." She turned her eyes to the window then, watching the white landscape pass by. "I truly want them to be that happy again, and yet, …"

"And yet?" Wesley pressed, his voice laced with tension.

Meeting his gaze once more, Christine sighed. "And yet, a part of me cannot help but think that love is like a worm on a fishing hook." Clearly confused, Wesley's brows rose into arches. "What I mean is that it is meant to lure you in, and once you are, you're pulled from the water and have your heart torn out."

Wesley snorted.

"What? Do you think this is funny?" she demanded, feeling her own resolve strengthened at the misery around her. She would truly be a fool to give away her heart!

78

"Your metaphor is a bit harsh, wouldn't you agree?"

Rolling her eyes, Christine shrugged. "Harsh or not, it is accurate."

"Do you truly believe that?" Wesley asked, his brows drawn down as though he could not believe what he'd heard.

Leaning back in her seat, Christine sighed. "I know that love can be beautiful. It's dazzling smiles and hidden looks, thudding hearts and passionate kisses. But," leaning forward, her voice hardened, and she raised her index finger, "that is only one of two faces. What about the other? Why do people constantly choose to ignore the ugly side of love?" Shaking her head, Christine snorted. "It is everywhere." Holding up one finger, she said, "Although they were happy once, now it looks as though William and Catherine have lost everything that's ever meant anything to them." Another finger came up. "The day I received your letter about William's accident, my friend Marianne told me that she believed her husband to be unfaithful. You should have seen the pain of dashed hopes in her eyes." Yet another finger rose. "And now, Eleanor is beside herself with misery because the man she loves has been deemed unsuitable by her mother and there is no future for them."

"Eleanor's in love?"

Christine's eyes went wide, and she clasped a hand over her mouth. "Bloody hell!" she cursed. "Why did you make me say that? I promised her not to breathe a word of this!"

Grinning, Wesley shook his head. "I didn't make you say anything, my dear. You—"

"My dear? I'm not your—"

"You were caught in a tirade of hatred," his eyebrows rose, and a crinkle came to his lips, "on the subject of love no less, which, I suppose, makes it ironic." Shaking his head, he met her gaze. "Do you want to know what I think?"

Christine's eyes narrowed. "Not particularly, considering that your opinion of me is never very flattering."

Wesley laughed. "Although we are alike in many ways—"

"We are?" Christine asked, crinkling her nose.

"Would you let me finish?"

"Fine." Gesturing for him to continue, Christine leaned back and tried her best to calm her thudding heart. This man was truly insufferable! What was she thinking fancying herself in love? Before their first year of marriage was out, they would kill each other.

"Although we are alike in many ways," Wesley continued, the corners of his mouth still drawn up in amusement, "we differ in one particular aspect."

"Which is?"

"Although I might not always admit it, I generally hope for the best," he said, holding her gaze. "I believe that things will work themselves out, and even if they don't, then happiness will come another way. You do the opposite."

Christine frowned. "What? Are you saying I hope for the worst? That doesn't make any sense!"

"I'm not saying you *hope* for the worst but you *expect* it." Leaning forward, he looked deep into her eyes. "You only see the risks, the dangers, the losses and the sadness. They carry more weight for you because in your opinion happiness is generally short-lived. It is only a matter of time before good will turn to bad, and you believe that if you ignore the good, then the bad will hurt less. Isn't that so?"

Christine took a slow breath as she stared into his blue eyes, so clear, and yet, so intense as she had never seen them. For once, his face was serious without the usual mischief that lurked somewhere in his eyes or in the curl of his lips. For once, she didn't feel as though he was teasing her.

Wesley swallowed. "Why is it that you're so dead set against marriage? Is it truly because you cannot guarantee how you'll feel in the years to come? Or because you're afraid of the pain it *might* bring?" Reaching out, he gently took her hand in his as his eyes continued to hold hers captive. "Hopes and wishes can be dashed even without a promise given," he warned, and a tinge of sadness clung to his voice that made her look at him with different eyes. "Should you find a man, who agrees to your…proposal," taking a deep breath, he swallowed before his teeth gritted together, "then what will protect you from losing your heart to him?" He shook his head. "Nothing will, and you will suffer the same or even worse for he will not feel responsible for your happiness because he never vowed to guard it as though it were his own."

"I have no intention of giving my heart to anyone," Christine whispered, her chilled hand warming in his gentle embrace.

Wesley laughed. "Only that is not your choice to make," he counselled. Then he took a deep breath, and a slight tremble shook his hands. "After all, I never intended to lose mine to you."

Her breath caught in her throat, and she found herself staring at him blatantly.

"It simply happened," he admitted, and a sheepish look came to his eyes that stole the breath from her lungs once more.

Never had Christine thought Wesley Everett to be a man who would declare his love to a woman who had made it clear that she had no intention of becoming his wife. After all, despite his slightly annoying sense of humour, he had always seemed like a reasonable man. And a reasonable man surely wouldn't...

And yet, he had. Hadn't he? Had he truly just told her that he loved her? Still staring at him, Christine tried to recall the words he had spoken. Had she misunderstood him?

"I just wanted you to know that," he whispered before releasing her hand. "I wanted you to know that the decisions you make will not only affect your own happiness," sitting back, he swallowed, "but mine as well."

As silence filled the carriage, Christine found herself frozen in place as though his words had turned her to stone. Her heart and mind felt numb, and it took every bit of strength she had left to force air down into her lungs.

What was happening? And more importantly, what was she to do now?

The remainder of the carriage ride back to Harrington Park passed in silence. However, as the horses turned down a familiar lane, Wesley turned to her and voiced his hopes that they would find William's eyes once more lit with the spark of love. He spoke lightly, and his face held none of the intense emotions Christine had seen there before. Had she only imagined them? Had he truly spoken to her of love?

Looking at him now, she could not help but doubt her own memories.

With her head held high, Christine did her best to ignore the tantalising tingles that swept through her as he helped her out of the carriage and up the front steps. They stepped into the foyer, ears listening, eyes searching their surroundings.

After welcoming them back, the butler gestured toward the front parlour, through which the occasional discordant note could be heard. Exchanging a strained, but still hopeful glance with her, Wesley strode forward to greet William and Catherine.

Staying back, Christine reminded herself of the role she had to play and carefully observed the colour draining from William's face as he jumped to his feet. Catherine, too, seemed flustered, and Christine felt her own heart rejoice at the sight of such obvious emotions.

Then William came toward her, his eyes meeting hers reluctantly as he bowed rather formally. "Welcome back," he said, a forced loudness to his voice that betrayed how uncomfortable he felt.

"Thank you," Christine whispered, then carefully raised her eyes to his. "I was rather hopeful when I received my sister's letter." Although the corners of her lips strained upward, Christine merely allowed a hint of a delighted smile. "Your request for my return led me to believe that there is still a future for us."

At her words, his mouth fell slightly open, and the tortured expression that came to his face told Christine everything she needed to know.

As the dark clouds that her sister's letter had conjured disappeared, Christine found herself determined to enjoy the time they had together. Always expecting the worst? Puh! She would show him!

Over supper, she chatted with her sister as well as Wesley, who would occasionally look at her with a warning in his eyes. However, reminded of the Christmas Ball that was to take place soon, she voiced her delight with the Christmas season in general as well as its enjoyments undeterred. Unable to contain her delight with her sister's situation—what did Wesley think of her *ludicrous* plan now?—Christine noticed William's confused glances with a hint of guilt. Still, she was unable to contain herself.

"I cannot wait for the Season to begin," she beamed, delighted with the distraction such an event would bring. "I need a completely new wardrobe, for these days I feel as though I have nothing to wear."

Wesley chuckled as his eyes swept over her in a fairly intimate fashion that reminded her of their entertaining banter at Sanford Manor. "If only that were true."

Unlike her, the brothers' mother was less than amused and completely failed to see the hilarity of the situation. "Wesley!" she chided. "Please refrain from such crude remarks at my table."

Clearing his throat, Wesley dropped his gaze. However, the tinge of red that came to his cheeks had Christine's heart hammering in her chest. "I apologise, Mother."

Guiding the conversation back to the Christmas Ball, Christine noticed with barely contained glee the absent look in William's eyes as he pretended not to stare at Catherine, who sat rather slumped in her chair, a touch of sorrow in her eyes. "We need to make a quick choice," she said, and his head snapped up as he noticed her looking at him. Ignoring the flustered expression that came to his face, she continued, "Thank goodness, we have our own seamstress in the house or we'd never have everything ready in time. We'll pick the masks first and then match the evening wear to them."

"Masks?" William croaked.

A hint of mischief in his eyes, Wesley frowned—so he had noticed as well, Christine thought. "Surely you remember that. After all, the earl's Christmas Ball has been a masque ball these past ten years."

"Yes, of course," William agreed. "Why do *you* not choose the masks?" he asked, turning to look at her. "My choice would probably not be well-received."

"Gladly," Christine agreed as happiness filled her heart, and for a moment, she closed her eyes in delight. "I cannot wait to dance the night away."

"Dancing," William whispered before he froze as all eyes turned to him. Clearing his throat, he straightened in his chair.

"Is something wrong?" his mother asked.

William shook his head. "I was simply wondering—with everything that I've forgotten—do I remember how to dance?"

Suppressing a chuckle, Christine smiled at him. What a glorious opportunity! "Do not worry, Dear. We'll practise. How about tomorrow?" She glanced at Wesley as well as her sister and rejoiced when no one objected. "How wonderful! Finally something to do!"

This was even more perfect than even she could have planned!

11

DANCE PRACTISE

For once, Wesley had to admit, Christine's plan truly had merit!

Although doubtful at first, he had instantly seen the familiar look of love shining in his brother's eyes whenever they fell on Catherine. To an outside observer, it was unmistakable! Could his brother be truly unaware of his feelings? Should they not simply tell him?

However, Christine had insisted that it would be too soon since they could not be certain how deep William's feelings were as of yet. Therefore, she had devised yet another plan to assure that William would fall in love with his wife all over again.

"Do you understand what you need to do?" Christine asked, eyeing him with a hint of doubt shining in her sparkling eyes.

Snorting, Wesley stepped in her path. "It's a simple enough plan."

"And yet, *you* didn't think of it," Christine mocked, a triumphant smile on her face as she took a step toward him, her chin raised. "Does this bother you?"

Delighted with the lightness that had returned to their communication—what had he been thinking confessing his love to her?—Wesley held her gaze. "Not at all," he said before his voice dropped to a whisper. "But do you believe it wise to have us dancing?" A frown came to her face. "Won't that make it harder for you to keep your hands off me?"

More or less all the women of his acquaintance would have blushed to the roots of their hair at such a remark, but not Christine. Instead, an amused smile came to her face before laughter spilled from her mouth. "Thank you for warning me," she whispered, her eyes daring him to say more. "I suppose your mother would be quite put out if I seduced you right there on the dance floor."

Wesley laughed. "I suppose it might be all she needed to finally disinherit me."

"Disinherit you?" Christine asked, a look of pure innocence on her face. "Why you? After all, you are just the innocent victim in this."

Shaking his head, he grinned at her, then took a step closer and his hands slid around her waist as though they belonged there.

A small gasp escaped her lips before the muscles in her jaw tensed and her eyes hardened. "Not now, Wes," she said teasingly, and yet, a touch of painful longing shook her voice. "You've made your choice, remember?" Stepping back, she pushed him away. "Now, go and make yourself useful. Get your brother and bring him to the ballroom." Then she turned on her heel and headed toward Catherine's bedchamber, mumbling, "Men! Unable to make up their minds! What is this world coming to?"

A wistful smile on his face, Wesley watched her disappear into her sister's room. Had he truly offended her by refusing her proposal? Was there any way for him to fix whatever had gone wrong between them? If only...

By now, there were too many *if only's*. Wesley couldn't even begin to sort through them, and so he turned down the other side of the corridor and retrieved his brother. Maybe if he helped with her plan, she would not think of him in an antagonistic way.

"I'm not certain that this is a good idea," William said some time later as he nervously danced from one foot onto the other. Meanwhile, their mother had taken her seat at the pianoforte in the large ballroom, her fingers flying over the keys.

"Believe me, it is," Wesley objected. A moment later, the door swung open, revealing the two sisters in its frame. Striding toward

BREE WOLF

them, Wesley greeted them with a formal bow. While Catherine smiled at him graciously, Christine rolled her eyes at him in a way that made him want to kiss her breathless. Instead, he said, "William appears rather nervous."

"Nervous?" Catherine asked, glancing at her husband, a hint of concern drawing down her brows. "Do you believe he truly forgot how to dance?"

Wesley smiled, then shook his head. "That's not what I meant. I assure you his nervousness has nothing to do with dancing."

Looking up at him, Catherine took a slow breath as a joyous smile lifted the corners of her mouth. "Truly?"

"Truly," Wesley assured her.

As they walked over to William, Wesley found Christine step around him, her hand slightly brushing his arm. "Thank you," she whispered as their eyes met, and he could see her appreciation for what he had done.

Before long, awkward silence once more lingered in the room until Christine called for a country dance and Wesley found himself standing up with Catherine as his mother began to play.

"Do not worry," Wesley counselled as he found Catherine's eyes stray to her husband again and again. "Your sister has a plan."

Laughing, Catherine turned her eyes to him. "As far as I can remember you've always been rather critical of her," she remarked, her dark green eyes searching his face. "You seem to have grown fond of her."

Wesley swallowed. "Well, she's…she's like no one else I've ever met."

A knowing smile came to Catherine's lips as they continued to twirl across the dance floor. They rehearsed dance after dance until toward the end of the cotillion, Christine's angry voice echoed across the dance floor. "Wesley!" Then she stormed toward him. "Wesley Everett, you are unbelievable!"

Momentarily stunned, Wesley swallowed before he remembered her plan as well as his role in it. Shrugging his shoulders, he apologised to Catherine all the while looking as embarrassed as he possibly could.

Lightning bolts shot from Christine's eyes as she fixed him with an icy stare; and yet, he thought to see a twinkle of amusement in her green depths. "My sister's poor feet! How can you be such a clumsy oaf?"

Forcing his face to remain unaffected by the amusement bubbling up in his chest, Wesley bowed his head in shame, watching Christine approach his brother as planned. "Dear," she said, her voice slightly apologetic. "I cannot have your brother continue to trample my sister's feet. Would you mind if we switched? I'm much more resilient in these matters."

Gritting his teeth, Wesley forced the laughter back down his throat. She was truly an actress to be admired!

"Certainly," his brother croaked, unspeakable relief shining in his eyes as he turned them to Catherine. How could anyone doubt the love he felt for her? Why was Christine insisting on continuing this charade?

"Splendid!" Coming toward him, a victorious smile on her face, Christine whispered, "This is going exactly as planned."

Again, they stood up for a cotillion.

"Clumsy oaf?" Wesley asked with raised brows as the steps brought them together.

"What?" Pretending to frown at him, Christine pressed her lips together as the corners of her mouth strove upward. "It was the spur of the moment. You are not truly saying that I've offended you, are you? I had no idea you were so sensitive where your dancing skills are concerned."

Shaking his head, Wesley laughed before he remembered where he was. However, neither William nor Catherine seemed to be aware of anything but each other. Only his mother cast him a disapproving frown.

When the music finally came to an end, Wesley waited, eyes expectantly trained on Christine. After all, she was the master mind behind this plan.

"How about a waltz?" she suggested, the look in her eyes an open challenge to his self-control.

Wesley swallowed, then glanced at his mother as she grumbled something unintelligible.

Unaffected, Christine strode over to the pianoforte, and after exchanging a few quick words, his mother turned back to the instrument and began to play.

Smiling at Christine in admiration, Wesley offered her his hand. As she took it, he pulled her close, delighted with the soft gasp that escaped her. "Have you thought this through?" he asked as he led her around the ballroom.

"Although you might not believe me," she snapped, a hint of annoyance in her voice, "my plans are always thought through. I do not make them up on a whim."

Smiling, Wesley shook his head. "I didn't mean your plan."

For a second, a frown drew down her brows before a disarming smile curled up her lips. "I see. Well, then let's just say I am willing to sacrifice my comfort in order to ensure my sister's happiness. Is that enough of an answer for you?"

"Your comfort?" Wesley mocked. "Is it such a burden to dance with me?"

Smiling, she shook her head at him. "What kind of an answer were you hoping for, Wes? That the feel of your hands on me is robbing me of every sense of right and wrong? That I'm about to lose control?"

Holding her gaze, Wesley shrugged. "Why not? It's how I feel." Then he froze. Had he truly just said that? Good God, what would she think of him now?

Staring up into Wesley's eyes, unguarded and brutally honest, Christine felt her knees go weak, and for a moment, she thought she would stumble. However, his arms held her, safe and warm, and guided her around the room without effort.

Who was this man? She wondered. Everything was fine, everything was going according to plan, and then he would say something like…and then she would feel as though…

Shaking her head to clear it, Christine forced a smile on her face. "Do not mock me, Wesley Everett," she croaked, hoping that her voice sounded less affected to his ears than it did to her own. "You only seek to unsettle me because you never believed I could be right. And now that William and Catherine are so close to falling in love all over again, you feel the need to put me in my place. Is that not so?" Swallowing, she forced her eyes up.

A smirk came to his face as he looked down at her, the initial hint of shock gone, replaced by the usual twinkle of amusement. "I apologise," he said, and her eyes narrowed. "Do not look so suspicious. Yes, you were right. There, I admit it. Can we move past this now? Not everything I say is meant as criticism. I wish you could believe that."

"But—" About to object, Christine stopped when the music came to an end.

Wesley bowed to her formally, then turned his head, and a smile lit up his face as he found William and Catherine still twirling around the dance floor. "Will!" he called his brother's name, who almost flinched before he turned around, eyes annoyed by the interruption. "What is it?" he snapped.

Wesley chuckled. "The music has stopped." He stepped toward his brother, whose face turned pink with embarrassment. "From where I stand, you're quite a talented dancer and in no need of further practise."

Forgotten was her own confusion at Wesley's renewed revelation as she watched her brother-in-law glance at her sister before his eyes shifted to her. He loved her. Christine knew it to be true the second he almost fled from the room.

Instantly, Wesley went after him.

"Is something wrong?" Catherine asked, her eyes big as she walked up to Christine. "I didn't notice…What happened? I don't understand. We were just dancing. Why would he—?"

Shaking her head, Christine hugged her sister. "The music had already ended, and you were still dancing." She pulled back and looked at her. "You didn't notice?"

Clasping both hands over her mouth, Catherine laughed. "I did not."

"Neither did he," Christine said. "Did I not tell you that you needed to dance with him? Mark my words: the Christmas Ball will solve all your problems."

Catherine frowned. "The Christmas Ball? Why is that?"

"Let me worry about that," Christine said, once again glancing at the door. "If you'll excuse me, I'll see what's going on." Then she strode from the ballroom in search of the brothers. For some reason, she couldn't keep still. She had to know what was going on.

As she came upon the parlour, voices echoed to her ear. Instantly, Christine stopped, then proceeded quietly until she stood with her ear pressed to the door that fortunately had been left ajar.

Inside, she could hear William pacing the floor, his shadow occasionally falling over the gap in the door. "Before we got married," he began, his voice strained as though he was at the end of his rope, "did you court Catherine as well?"

Christine frowned. Why was William jealous of his brother?

"What?" Wesley's voice cut through the room. "What gave you that idea?" Although he sounded honestly surprised, Christine thought to detect a hint of guilt in his voice.

"I don't know. You look at her as though…"

A moment of silence hung over the room, and Christine finally realised that she had misunderstood. William accused his brother of having feelings for her, Christine, because he believed her, Christine, to be his wife and…Drat! This whole plan was truly confusing!

"As though what?" Wesley pressed, his voice calm once more.

Listening intently, Christine waited. What would Wesley tell his brother? He couldn't possibly confess his feelings even if they were true? But were they? She couldn't help but wonder.

"As though you care for her," William finished, a clear question ringing in his voice.

"Of course, I care for her," Wesley confirmed. "She's family. She's my sister-in-law."

That was not exactly what Christine wanted to hear, and yet, she understood that he couldn't possibly tell the truth. Whatever it was!

Again, William paced the floor. "You don't look at her like a brother does," he insisted. "You look at her the way I…" He broke off.

Another moment of silence hung about the room before hurried footsteps came toward her. By instinct, Christine jumped aside.

A moment later, William came storming out of the parlour. Not seeing her, he rushed up the stairs to his chamber.

12

A PROPOSAL REPEATED

*T*he next few days passed rather quickly as Christine was busy with preparations for the Christmas Ball. Since Catherine was too preoccupied with thoughts of her husband and neither of the brothers nor their mother showed any interest in readying their wardrobe for the night in question, Christine graciously took it upon herself to choose masks and matching gowns for her sister as well as herself.

Although the dowager countess was always well informed, she tended to stay indoors whenever the temperatures dropped to allow for snow and could not be persuaded to change her mind with regard to the Christmas Ball.

It was just as well. Christine thought. She'd rather not have the old woman's watchful eyes criticising her every move.

Despite the general merriment of the season, Christine had to admit that the dream-like glow that had come to her sister's face during the dance rehearsal was dimming. Although clearly falling in love with Catherine, William seemed to keep his distance, mostly avoiding their company wherever he could. In consequence, Catherine's mood sank.

Until one morning.

Coming down the stairs, Christine found her sister at the piano-forte, playing a merry tune, an almost face-splitting smile on her lips. "What happened?" Christine asked, rushing over.

As Catherine's glowing eyes turned to her, she felt certain that all would be well. "He kissed me," her sister whispered, eyes shifting from side to side to ensure that they were alone.

"He did?" Christine gasped, then she pulled her sister into a tight embrace and held her close. "How? When?"

"Last night," Catherine mumbled, tears of joy clinging to her eye-lashes. "I couldn't sleep, and so I went down into the kitchen. He found me there and offered to help. I suppose he couldn't sleep, either."

Christine snorted. "Or he saw you leave and followed you."

"Do you truly think so?"

"It wouldn't surprise me at all," Christine said vehemently. "Did I not tell you that he would lose his heart to you all over again?"

A slight shadow fell over Catherine's face.

"What is it?"

Her sister shrugged, then walked over to the window and looked out at the snow. "I'm never quite certain if he truly does love me or if he only…"

"Desires you?" Christine asked, seeing Wesley's wicked grin before her mind's eye as she spoke so boldly.

A slight blush came to her sister's face, but she nodded. "How can I be certain? Of course, he hasn't said anything about love. How could he? He believes me to be his—"

Footsteps echoed closer, and a moment later, William stepped into the parlour.

Obviously surprised to see them, his face paled and he stammered an apology before fleeing the room.

While Catherine's face held a hint of sorrow, Christine laughed. "He loves you," she whispered, grasping her sister's hands. "I'm certain of it, and soon you will be, too."

The next few days passed in fairly the same fashion. While Christine was busy with preparations, William and Catherine skulked around the house with hanging heads and wistful eyes, overjoyed to see the other, and yet, afraid to remain in the other's company for too long. Sometimes, Christine felt the need to clunk their heads together in order to make them see what was so obvious. How could they not know? How could they not be certain of the other's feelings?

"You seem to be enjoying yourself," Wesley observed as he stepped into the parlour, his eyes gliding over the different kinds of fabric spread out over the settee as well as the two armchairs.

Christine shrugged. "I like being in charge," she admitted, then raised her gaze to meet his. "Were you not aware of that?"

Wesley chuckled. "Not at all. It comes as quite the surprise for me," he teased before his face sobered and he sat down next to her, pushing aside a roll of fabric. "Can I assume you run your parents' household with the same firm hand?"

Christine sighed. "In that case, you'd actually assume wrong."

His eyebrows rose in surprise.

"My parents' house is my mother's domain," she explained with a wistful smile. "She is too much like me and would never willingly relinquish control."

Wesley laughed. "She sounds like a delightful creature."

Rolling her eyes at him, Christine said, "You might be of a different opinion if you had to share your life with a woman like that. Because a woman like that—"

"A woman like you?"

"—would not simply run your household, she would run your life."

A gentle smile came to his face as he looked at her. "That sounds very appealing."

Christine snorted. "Wesley, please, you know as well as I do that you like to get your way. You like the idea of bowing your head to another as little as I do."

"Why does anyone have to bow their head?" he asked, a somewhat incredulous look in his blue eyes. "Can we not both stand tall together?"

Christine sighed. "I suppose it's possible, but extremely rare."

A smile curled his lips as his eyes swept over her in admiration. "You're a rare woman," he whispered before a mischievous sparkle lit up his eyes, "and I like to believe that I'm a somewhat unusual man myself."

Christine laughed. "You are indeed, Wesley Everett." She rose from the settee, feeling the need to put a little distance between them for the way he looked at her was truly unsettling. "However, you know as well as I do that we are not a good match." Turning to face him, she shook her head. "We are not the kind of people who commit for a lifetime."

"But does that not speak in our favour?" he asked, abandoning his seat and coming toward her. "That we are of equal mind on this?"

Taking a deep breath, Christine eyed him critically as he approached, noting with a hint of concern the decrease in distance between them. "Are we?"

"Do you truly believe what you say?" he asked, a frown on his face. "Or are you just looking for reasons not to accept my proposal?"

Christine swallowed as his eyes held hers. Had he truly meant it?

"Marry me," he whispered, "and I'll gladly let you run my household as well as my life."

Shaking her head, Christine tried her best to ignore the thudding of her heart as well as the delightful tingles his words trailed all over her body. "You do not mean what you say," she said firmly, willing him as well as herself to believe it. "You only speak the way you do because …because you…you," she licked her lips as he came closer, his eyes drilling into hers, "because you want me all to yourself."

"I do want you all to myself," he whispered as his arms came around her, pulling her against him. "I have from the moment we met."

As his warm breath brushed over her skin and his eyes told her more than he could possibly say, Christine didn't know what to think or do or feel because in that moment it was as though they merged into one being and she couldn't even say where he ended and she began.

His hands tightened on her back, pressing her closer against him, as his head bent down to hers, his eyes searching her face before they dipped lower.

"Have you seen my brother?" William's voice echoed through the half-open door.

Harrington's butler cleared his throat. "I believe he's in the parlour."

At their voices, Wesley tensed, a low growl rising from his throat, before he stepped back. As his hands released her, Christine felt a stab of regret and she saw a matching expression cross over his face as well.

"Wesley, are you—?" William stuck his head in the door, but stopped the moment he perceived them. His eyes shifted over their faces, and Christine could have sworn she saw a glimmer of suspicion.

Fortunately, though, he did not act upon it.

Instead, a mask of polite indifference came to his face as he greeted them.

Knowing that uncomfortable silence was to follow, Christine quickly excused herself and fled the room. After everything that had happened, she needed a moment to herself.

With a sigh, she ascended the stairs. Now, she could not pretend that Wesley had not meant his proposal, but had only spoken in the heat of the moment. Now, his intentions had been quite clear.

Now, she would have to refuse him…or not?

13

THE CHRISTMAS BALL

y the time the day of the Christmas Ball finally came, Wesley only wanted it to be over. Although he had to admit that Christine's charade had been somewhat entertaining in the beginning, now it felt almost suffocating to not be himself, at least, not completely. He could not imagine how the two sisters felt, considering that they had to pretend to be the other.

Wesley shook his head. This had gone too far, and no matter what happened at the ball, the charade would end tonight.

To his surprise, Christine sought him out a mere hour before they were to depart for the ball and enlisted his help as well as her sister's for yet another one of her daring plans. Only this time, it involved his friend's sister Eleanor as well as the girl's secret love Henry Waltham!

When he had first realised her intentions, Wesley had refused to have any part in the plan, and yet, now, as he found himself walking into the earl's home, Catherine dressed in a flattering dark green dress on his arm, his eyes scanned the crowd, looking for said Henry Waltham.

Had he truly agreed to this? Again, he shook his head, and a soft chuckle escaped him. Had he not told her he would be delighted to allow her to run his life? Should he truly be surprised that she would do so without even accepting his proposal?

"Are you all right?" Catherine asked, glancing up at him. "You seemed somewhat displeased when Christine shared her idea with us."

"Shared her idea?" he mumbled, once again shaking his head in disbelief. "She did not share her idea. She all but told us what to do without so much as asking whether we were inclined to do so."

Catherine smiled. "Would you have refused her?"

Wesley sighed. "No." For a moment, his eyes lingered on Christine as she walked through the throng of guests on his brother's arm before they caught sight of the very man Christine had them looking for. "There he is," Wesley said, inconspicuously inclining his head to the right end of the refreshment table. "At least, I believe it's him. With the mask, it's not easy to be certain. However, he has the Waltham build. So, I suppose it could be him."

"It could be him?" Catherine chuckled, her own worries temporarily suspended by Christine's newest concoction. Then she turned her head, and her voice sobered. "And there is Eleanor with her mother," she added, gesturing to the left end of said table. "Does the mask not look exactly like the one Christine described?"

Wesley shrugged, glad that Catherine was by his side for he could not for the life of him remember what the bloody thing ought to look like. However, what was even more telling than the mask was the fact that young Henry Waltham couldn't seem to keep his eyes off Eleanor.

"Aw, the poor girl looks miserable. Where is Lord Stanhope?" Catherine looked around before catching sight of him as he came walking over.

"Good evening, dear friend," Lord Stanhope greeted them with a slight incline of his head. "Your sulking face I would recognise anywhere." An amused curl to his lips, his friend then turned his gaze to Catherine and his eyes seemed to narrow. "Christine Dansby, I presume." His voice held a questioning tone as his gaze returned to Wesley.

Shrugging, Wesley held his inquisitive stare. "For now."

"I see," Lord Stanhope mumbled. "Do I dare ask what you've planned for tonight?"

Closing his eyes for a moment, Wesley simply shook his head. How was he to know? After all, it was not *his* plan!

"I see that your sister and mother have accompanied you tonight, my lord," Catherine said as she glanced over to the two ladies in question.

"Indeed," Lord Stanhope replied, his eyes still shifting back and forth between them clearly in the hopes of unveiling their secret plans. "Would you care to join us for a refreshment? I'm certain my sister would be overjoyed to see you again," he suggested politely before a hint of sarcasm came to his voice. "After all, during the week you spent with us, the two of you were nearly inseparable."

While Wesley graciously or at least as graciously as he could accepted his friend's invitation, Catherine averted her eyes, a suppressed smile on her lips.

Following Lord Stanhope, they bid the ladies a good evening. While Eleanor seemed genuinely delighted, Lady Stanhope merely gave them a curd nod and mumbled something that *could* have been a greeting—however, Wesley was glad he hadn't been listening too closely.

With a glance at Christine and William, who were just then speaking to Robert Dashwood and his new wife—Robert had been quite changed since the last time Wesley had seen him!—Wesley procured a glass of wine for Catherine before forcing his attention toward Lady Stanhope. Curse Christine and her ludicrous plans!

"This is truly a marvellous event," he beamed, hoping his voice sounded genuine. "It reminds me of that New Year's Ball at Stanhope Grove, was it three years ago?"

"Four," Lady Stanhope offered, and from one second to the next, her sour expression slid off her face. "It truly was, wasn't it?" she trilled, her eyes distant as she clutched her hands before her chest like a young girl. "I admit I have long since thought to host another such ball."

"Oh, what a wonderful notion!" Wesley exclaimed enthusiastically, which earned him a confused look from his friend. However, all that mattered was that with Lady Stanhope's attention diverted, Catherine could use the opportunity to steer Eleanor away...and into the arms of young Henry Waltham.

Trying to follow Lady Stanhope's raptures about their legendary New Year's Ball as well as her ideas for another equally impressive event, Wesley found his thoughts wandering to the one woman who was at the root of all of this.

Currently, Christine was twirling around the dance floor in his brother's arms, and although Wesley knew better than anyone that neither one of them had any romantic intentions toward the other, he could not help but feel a tinge of displeasure. How much worse would he feel if Christine actually made good on her promise...or rather threat...and take a lover?

In that moment, Wesley felt certain he would die on the spot...or rather that he would kill the *lucky* man without thinking about it twice!

"Would you not agree?" Lady Stanhope asked, her eyes looking at him as she waited for an answer.

Wesley swallowed as he had no idea what the lady was talking about. However, her demeanour suggested that a favourable answer would be most agreeable to her, and so Wesley nodded his head vigorously. "Absolutely, my lady. There is no question."

A satisfied smile came to Lady Stanhope's face, and Wesley found himself relax before his eyes drifted across the room where Henry Waltham was just then leading Eleanor into the ballroom. "If you'll excuse me?" he asked, then bowed to Lady Stanhope as well as his friend and quickly departed.

"Did everything go as planned?" he whispered to Catherine as he came to stand beside her, eyes following the young couple as they took their places on the dance floor beside Christine and William.

Catherine nodded. "I think she did notice that I was not...myself," she whispered, an amused smile on her lips. "But her excitement overruled any suspicions she might have had. Are they not adorable?"

Lost in each other's eyes, Eleanor and Henry floated on air across the dance floor, completely unaware of the world around them. "They remind me of you and William," Wesley said with a smile.

Catherine drew in a steadying breath before she nodded her head. "I can only hope..."

"I know," Wesley mumbled as he noticed his brother craning his neck, his eyes searching for something...or rather someone. Wesley chuckled. Most likely, for the woman by his side.

"I'm glad Christine made us do this," Catherine said, her eyes shifting back and forth between the beaming couple and the man she loved. "I cannot imagine why her mother would oppose the match. Henry is a good man. He's not like his brothers. And seeing your child happy should be more important than...anything."

Drawing in a slow breath, Wesley nodded, bracing himself for what was to come. Then he offered Catherine his hand and led her into the ballroom.

Only a moment later, the dance ended and the music stopped, and under the mistletoe in the centre of the room stood Eleanor and Henry, eyes aglow with happiness while their cheeks burned with embarrassment.

Under the encouragement of the surrounding guests, Eleanor and Henry exchanged a quick kiss. Unfortunately, it was a far cry from the kind of kiss a couple in love would have dreamed of. However, it would have to do.

Once more offering Catherine his hand, Wesley led her onto the dance floor, and they stood up for a cotillion, William and Christine only two couples down from them.

"He's staring at you," Wesley whispered, trying his best to suppress the laughter that threatened.

Blushing slightly, Catherine glanced at her husband. "He is, isn't he?" she whispered back. "I only wish I knew why."

"Because he loves you," Wesley replied, a hint of exasperation in his voice. If only they had all spoken their minds from the very beginning, none of this would have been necessary! Curse Christine and her ludicrous plans!

"Do you truly believe so?"

"I know so," Wesley insisted for it was all but written on his brother's face.

When the dance ended, Wesley pulled Catherine's hand through the crook of his arm and led her across the dance floor without delay. "Will," he called, and his face split into a big grin. "I've come to trade."

Rolling her eyes at him, Christine slapped him playfully on the arm, a spark of amusement in her eyes as she snapped, "What a crude remark! I certainly understand your mother's relief that you're not the first-born son."

Putting a pained expression on his face, Wesley clutched his chest as though mortally injured. "You wound me, my lady." Then he bowed to her. "May I have this dance, nonetheless?"

"You may," Christine said graciously and took his hand, "although you do not deserve it."

As he led her away, Wesley couldn't help but laugh—although he tried to do it as inconspicuously as he possibly could.

"Would you care to enlighten me as to what brought on this rather inappropriate behaviour?" Christine asked with an air of mock indignation.

Grinning, Wesley pulled her close as the orchestra began to play the first notes of a waltz. "You should've been an actress," he whispered as his thumb gently brushed over the back of her hand, "for you're truly amazing."

Holding his gaze, she took a slow breath, all amusement leaving her face. "Is that a compliment?"

"Nothing but," he assured her.

Uncharacteristically touched, Christine nodded before her eyes left his and she gazed over his shoulder. "Do you think it will work?"

In no doubt whatsoever with regard to whom she was referring to, Wesley nodded. "Did you forget that it was your plan?"

"Even the best plans can fail," she conceded, a rather sheepish grin on her face, "…sometimes."

"He loves her," Wesley said, holding her gaze. "Even a blind man could see it."

"I know." A soft smile came to her lips. "Thank you for your help. Eleanor looked truly happy when Henry led her onto the dance floor. As did he."

"You're welcome," Wesley said, and his hands tightened on her.

Surprised, she met his gaze, a hint of confusion in them as she searched his face.

Wesley swallowed. "You still haven't given me an answer."

As her gaze dropped from his, she took a deep breath, and a slight tremble shook her body. "Wesley, I…I…"

As the last notes of the waltz evaporated into thin air, Christine lifted her head and met his gaze…before she stepped back and turned her attention to the centre of the room.

For a moment, Wesley closed his eyes as exhaustion washed over him. Was this truly a futile attempt? Was there any way for him to win her hand? Or was he simply fooling himself?

Then excited murmurs drew his attention from his inner turmoil, and following Christine's line of view, he found his brother standing under the mistletoe in the centre of the large ballroom…Catherine by his side—the way it ought to be.

For a moment, they seemed lost in each other's eyes, and Wesley wondered if the love that existed between them could ever exist between Christine and himself. Had she ever looked at him like that? Had he? He honestly could not say. His heart, however, ached for it, and he knew, just like Catherine, he could not give up.

Glancing at the surrounding audience a bit uneasily, William pulled Catherine closer before he leaned down and kissed her the way a husband would kiss his wife. However, their audience at large had no idea that they were in fact husband and wife, and so it was not long before whispers of outrage echoed through the vaulted room. Eyes narrowed, and frowns appeared on a number of faces. Glancing at Christine, whose eyes also took in the change in the air, Wesley swallowed as the atmosphere slowly shifted from jolly delight to hostile accusation.

"What now?" he whispered to her.

Without answering him, she took a few steps closer to the couple under the mistletoe.

When they finally broke their kiss and a sense of shocked reality returned to their eyes, Christine strode forward without a moment's hesitation. "Isn't this a marvellous night?" she beamed as confused eyes turned to her...after all, as far as the rest of the assembly was concerned, she was William's wife.

Unimpressed, Christine raised her hands and removed her mask...and just as quickly, open hostility was replaced by stunned silence before delighted laughter echoed through the room.

Then Christine turned and looked at Catherine, gesturing for her to remove her mask as well, and with a hesitant look at William, she did so.

Instantly, the room erupted in smiles and laughter, compliments and praise.

"Wonderful!"

"What a marvellous idea!"

"Did anyone notice they'd switched places?"

Eyes fixed on his brother, Wesley swallowed as William's eyes narrowed and his face turned pale. Had he already understood the full meaning of what had just been revealed to him? Wesley wished he knew what his brother thought in that very moment. He could only hope that one day he would be able to look back at this day and laugh as well.

Suddenly the centre of attention, Christine saw the strain on her sister's as well as brother-in-law's face as the other guests crowded around them, eager to exchange a word or offer their congratulations on such a marvellous idea.

Trying her best to shield them, Christine was beyond grateful when Wesley called for the carriage and directed them out the door with a sure hand.

And yet, after the loud hustle-bustle at the earl's ball, the silence that fell over them in the small confines of the carriage felt even heavier. Although Christine and Wesley tried to explain, William barely paid them any attention.

Looking at her sister, Christine found her almost shivering in her seat, fear clearly edged in her eyes as she uneasily glanced at her husband.

At a loss for the first time in her life, Christine walked over the threshold into the front hall of Harrington Park, her mind frantically searching for a way to make William understand that it had never been their intention to deceive him. Would he ever forgive her sister? Would Catherine ever forgive her?

Spinning on her heel, Christine looked from William to Catherine. "Let us sit and talk about this," she suggested, panic in her voice as the full meaning of what she had done finally dawned on her.

Then she stepped into the parlour, raking her mind for the right words to explain that... Again, she shook her head. What else could she possibly say? How could she make William understand and ensure that her sister's heart would not be broken for the second time since her husband's accident?

"Maybe we should leave them alone," Wesley suggested as he stepped into the parlour behind Catherine and William.

"But—"

"We should go," he insisted, his eyes gentle as he took her by the elbow and led her out of the room. "They need time alone."

Christine cast one last look at her sister's miserable face before the door closed and Wesley led her up the stairs. "What if he cannot forgive her?"

"He loves her."

"Yes, but what if he cannot forgive her?" Christine insisted, leaning heavily on Wesley's arm as all strength seemed to leave her. "What if—?"

"Even if he does not forgive her right now," Wesley interrupted, turning down the corridor toward Christine's room, "he will eventually. Sometimes, things take time. We'll need to be patient."

Gnawing on her lower lip, Christine grumbled, "I hate that. I've never been patient. Waiting is like torture."

A soft smile came to Wesley's face as they stopped in front of her door. "Then you know how I feel."

Holding his gaze for a moment, Christine swallowed, knowing only too well what he was referring to. "Maybe we should go downstairs and see what's going on," she suggested, desperate to return to their former topic of conversation. After all, it was much safer. "Maybe they need us. Maybe—"

Shaking his head, Wesley stepped in her way as she started down the corridor. "They need time alone, and you need rest."

"Don't be ridiculous!" Christine snapped, trying to brush by him. "It was my plan, my doing, I cannot just go to bed and leave my sister alone to answer for all of this." With every word, her voice was growing more panicky, and Wesley's hands tightened on her arms to keep her from running off. "She needs me. I'm her sister. We've always done everything together. I cannot leave her alone now. She needs me. I—"

Determination hardened his features, and in the next instant, his mouth came down on hers, silencing her.

Lost in her rambling, Christine had not seen it coming, but it had been the very thing she'd needed. Her arms rose to his shoulders, then snaked around his neck, pulling her closer against him as she kissed him with the same passion that echoed in his heart.

Her mind instantly abandoned all thoughts of her sister and brother-in-law, and all she could think about was the last time they'd kissed. It had been too long since then. Why had they waited this long?

Wesley's arms held her tightly as he walked her backwards until her back came to rest against the door to her bedchamber. Heat burned in her body as his hands touched her and his mouth devoured hers.

Gasping for breath, Christine clung to him. "Have you changed your mind?" she whispered as her lips sought his once more.

Instantly, his hands stilled, and he pulled back, his jaw tense as he held her gaze. Then he swallowed, regret clearly edged in his eyes, and took a step back, his hands releasing their hold on her. "I have not," he said, drawing in a slow breath. "Have you?"

Feeling the same emotions well up in her chest that she could so plainly read on his face, Christine shook her head. "I can't marry you, Wesley."

"Why not?" He gritted his teeth as his eyes burned into hers. "Do you not…care for me?"

Christine swallowed, knowing that she cared for him a lot more than she would ever allow herself to admit. "I never wanted to get married because I know it would not make me happy." She shrugged apologetically as the look on his face slowly broke her heart. "It's not part of the plan. It never was," she whispered, forcing back the tears that threatened.

Although she had expected regret, confusion or even anger, Christine was not surprised to see a gentle smile come to his face as he took a step toward her. "Maybe you need a new plan," he said, softly taking her hands in his. "Things change, Chris," involuntarily, her heart skipped a beat as he called her by the nickname that had always made her feel special, "life changes. Do not reject me simply because I'm not part of your plan." He held her gaze, and his hands closed more tightly around hers. "Reject me if you do not want me." He swallowed, then took a step back and released her hands. "Think about it." Reaching around her, he opened the door to her chamber. "Good night," he whispered, taking another step backwards, "and I swear I'll drag you back up here on your hair if I find you anywhere near the parlour."

Christine laughed, and her heart instantly felt lighter. "I promise I'll not venture downstairs. There. Satisfied?"

A gleam in his eyes, he shook his head. "Far from it, but it's a start."

14

A BROTHER'S ADVICE

lthough Christine had not accepted his proposal, she had not declined it, either…at least, not in the strictest sense, and so Wesley found himself sitting across from her at the breakfast table the next morning with a hopeful heart.

And yet, despite every encouragement he had whispered to himself in the dark of night, the early morning light brought back all the doubts and confusion that he couldn't seem to banish. Where would they go from there? Especially now, that their charade was over.

No matter what the future held for William and Catherine, Wesley would soon return to his townhouse and Christine, he presumed, would return to her parents' house. Soon, their ways would part. What then? What would she do? Would she…?

Wesley gritted his teeth as he eyed Christine, who seemed to have shaken off the previous night without difficulty. In that moment, he envied her ability to recover from whatever plagued her in a matter of hours.

Even though last night she had seemed on the brink of tears, afraid to admit that she did in fact care for him, this morning found her smiling, her eyes aglow with delight as she glanced at him. Was she enjoying the tortured expression that undoubtedly shone on his face? Was she only biding her time until he would finally give in?

Would he?

Hanging his head, Wesley couldn't be certain. If she made good on her *threat*, would he ultimately accept her proposal in order to ensure that no one else received an invitation into her bed?

By the time his brother and Catherine finally came down to breakfast, Wesley was no closer to an answer. To his delight, though, one look at the smiling couple, who couldn't seem to keep their hands off each other, told them that he had been right. William loved Catherine, and no matter how hurt he had been by their charade, he had had no choice but to forgive her.

If only Wesley could be certain that Christine loved him! There had been signs, and yet, he was far from certain. Was that how Catherine had felt with regard to her husband's love? If it was, he felt for her even more than before for this was pure agony!

After breakfast, while the ladies once more discussed the Christmas Ball, William approached his brother. "Since I don't remember, I need to ask." He glanced at Christine. "Has there ever been anything between the two of you?"

Wesley cleared his throat. Apparently, his brother could read him as well as Wesley had read William's feelings for Catherine.

"When I thought she was my wife," his brother continued, "I would occasionally come upon the two of you and wonder why I didn't feel jealous because considering the way you looked at each other, any husband should." A compassionate look in his eyes, his brother leaned closer. "If you care for her, then fight for her."

Feeling exhausted, Wesley shook his head. "She is determined not to marry."

"Maybe," William said, an encouraging smile on his face. "But look at me, there is nothing that is not possible where love is concerned."

Wesley nodded. If only he knew if she loved him. However, he didn't dare ask, afraid the answer would shatter him.

And so he kept his distance, hoping and wondering, but ultimately realising that there was very little if anything at all that he could do. If she was determined not to marry, then there was no future for the two of them.

Although he had known that both of them would leave Harrington Park soon, Wesley was stunned to come downstairs a few days
after the Christmas Ball and find her luggage in the hall.

Pulling on her coat, Christine smiled at her sister, then hugged her
fiercely, whispering something in her ear.

The hint of tears stood in Catherine's eyes, and she blinked rapidly
as she returned her sister's embrace.

"She decided to return to London," William said, coming to stand
beside his brother.

As his heart thudded painfully in his chest, Wesley gritted his
teeth. "Why?" he almost growled as the meaning of her departure hit
him with full force.

William shrugged, his eyes carefully watching Wesley's face. "She
said she wanted to give us space to reacquaint yourselves with each
other."

Feeling his brother's watchful gaze on him, Wesley swallowed.
"Well, I suppose she's right." He forced his eyes from Christine and
turned to face his brother. "Maybe I should head back to Town as
well."

A slow smile came to William's face. "Are you going after her?"

"No." Shaking his head, Wesley glanced at the woman who held
his heart. "She's made her feelings perfectly clear."

William sighed. "Trust me. You will never forgive yourself if you
give up now. Even if it seems hopeless, anyone could tell that she cares
for you."

Wesley's head snapped up.

"Did you not know?" William asked, nodding his head, a smile on
his face. "I suppose people are difficult to read when you're personally
involved, is that not so?"

Wesley nodded, wishing he could see what was right in front of
him without his own fears and doubts clouding the image.

"You should at least bid her farewell," his brother suggested before he walked over to his wife, drawing her aside.

Swallowing, Wesley did as suggested. He drew in a slow breath,
forcing his features not to betray the turmoil that he felt inside as he
approached the rather disinterested woman pulling on her gloves.
"You're leaving."

Slowly, her head rose, and yet, another second passed before she
met his eyes. "I am," she confirmed, a slight quiver in her lip as she
spoke. "There's no point in prolonging the inevitable."

Frowning, Wesley searched her face.

As she saw him looking, a big smile spread over her face, covering the sadness that rested in her dark green eyes. "It always saddens me to part ways with my sister," she rushed to explain, "however, I suppose they need time alone right now. And I have to admit I long to return to London. After all, the new season is soon to start, and I have yet to choose a new wardrobe."

A soft smile came to Wesley's face as he realised the effort it took her to speak as cheerfully as she did, and although she blamed her emotions on bidding her sister goodbye, Wesley felt certain that at least part of the tears that threatened were meant for him. "Thank you for all you did," he said, taking a step closer, his eyes holding hers. "William and Catherine are happy again, and although I hate to admit it, it wouldn't have happened if it hadn't been for your…ludicrous plan."

Her eyes narrowed. "Ludicrous plan?"

Ignoring her, Wesley smiled. "I'll miss you," he whispered, and her brows went up in surprise. "Without you, life will seem dull. How will I ever fill my days without being pressured into lending a hand with a variety of insane ideas?"

"Insane ideas?"

"Call on me," Wesley said, "if you ever need help leading another couple to their happily-ever-after."

Christine nodded. "I shall." She took a slow breath. "Goodbye, Wes. It's been a pleasure," she whispered, a mischievous twinkle in her eyes.

Wesley smiled. "It has been indeed."

Then she turned and stepped over the threshold into the cold winter air toward the waiting carriage that would take her back to London and away from him.

15

A NEW SEASON

Only a fortnight into the new year with the Season just beginning, Christine found herself bored beyond all measure. Although assembling a new wardrobe had been mildly entertaining, it had still been overshadowed by a highly inconvenient sense of loss.

At every outing, be it a play, a ball or merely a stroll in the park, Christine did not primarily pay attention to those who attended, but instead markedly noted the one man who did not. Was he still at Harrington Park? She wondered, unable to concentrate on the Earl of Carrington's rather boring narration of his travels to the continent.

"On the voyage back, the ship was hit by a terrible storm," he recounted, his eyes sparkling with triumph as though he had just returned from battle, "and for most of the night, it seemed as though it would not be able to withstand such forces."

"Goodness," Christine exclaimed as her eyes inconspicuously scanned the ballroom for anyone remotely interesting. "You must have been terrified."

The earl shrugged. "I suppose I was a bit alarmed, but mostly for the delay it would cause with regard to our arrival in London. After all, I had commitments I did not wish to go back on."

"What a marvellous tale," Christine said, hoping she didn't sound as bored as she was. "I'm certain my parents would long to hear it." She gestured to the left where her parents stood, a glass of wine in their hands, observing their daughter with interest.

"Certainly," the earl exclaimed and willingly followed her, greeting her parents with exuberant delight that had Mrs. Dansby look at her daughter with questioning eyes.

Seeing her mother's line of thinking, Christine unobtrusively shook her head, and the glow in her mother's eyes vanished. Even if the fate of the world hung in the balance, she would never agree to marry the Earl of Carrington of all people!

However, desperate to rid herself of him, Christine was more than willing to discuss her views on marriage with her disapproving mother yet again.

When both her parents' as well as the earl's attention was no longer directed at her, Christine quietly excused herself, voicing her desire for a refreshment. Strolling around the ballroom, hearing people laugh and chat, seeing couples dance and smile at each other, Christine could not help but remember the Christmas Ball. It had been a truly marvellous night, and as though her thoughts had conjured her, she turned a corner and came face to face with Eleanor.

Instantly, the young girl's solemn face vanished, and a deep smile came to her lips as she stepped forward. "Christine!" she beamed. "How wonderful to see you here."

Delighted to see Eleanor again, Christine greeted her, ignoring the girl's mother, who eyed her with a hint of disapproval. Lord Stanhope, however, politely inclined his head to her.

"I am just as glad," Christine replied honestly. "To tell you the truth, I've been quite bored. Come, tell me how you've been." Drawing Eleanor away from her mother's watchful eyes, Christine guided her toward the large window front. "How is Henry?" she whispered.

Eleanor's eyes opened in alarm as she glanced over her shoulder at her mother. "I haven't seen him since the Christmas Ball," she admitted, sadness returning to her eyes. "Mother was quite put out when she saw us kiss." A hint of remorse rang in Eleanor's voice, and yet, her eyes sparkled with the memory of that night. "But I cannot regret what happened. It was like a dream. Thank you," she said emphatically.

"Thank you for making it happen. If it hadn't been for you, we never even could have danced."

"It was my pleasure," Christine assured her before her voice became serious. "Is your mother still insisting on a *suitable* match?"

Eleanor nodded. "More so than ever. I do believe she suspects I might do something foolish, which is why she is ever watchful these days."

Glancing over Eleanor's shoulder, Christine found the girl's mother following their every move. "I'm sorry to hear that. I suspect you have not found anyone to your liking."

Sadly, Eleanor shook her head. "No one even compares to Henry."

Christine nodded as the face of a certain gentleman drifted before her inner eye. "I know what you mean," she mumbled deflatedly before calling herself to reason. "Life is what it is," she spoke out vehemently, momentarily startling Eleanor. "We ought to be out on the dance floor, enjoying ourselves, not because we are in search of a husband but because it is better than standing here and wasting away."

A hesitant smile on her face, Eleanor nodded. "Maybe you're right."

Christine squeezed her hand in encouragement, and before long, they both found themselves on the dance floor, willing away the loneliness that threatened to engulf them.

Smiling at each other from across the room here and there, the two women found barely an opportunity to speak again as they spent the remainder of the evening dancing with a variety of gentlemen. While Eleanor did her best to be cheerful, Christine could see the effort it took her to maintain the polite smile that rested on her face. Lady Stanhope, though, glowed with delight, probably counting the days until her daughter would be properly married.

"You seem distracted," Viscount Eastwood observed, his sharp eyes trailing over her face.

Forcing her attention back to him, Christine smiled. "I apologise, my lord. I...well, I cannot explain without betraying someone's confidence."

To her surprise, he laughed, mischief dancing in his eyes. "Your friend seems quite miserable," he observed as his eyes shifted to Eleanor, "despite her effort to appear cheerful."

Glancing at her dance partner through narrowed eyes, Christine said, "I was being too obvious, was I not?"

He shrugged, a good-natured smile on his face. "You were quite discreet, I assure you. However, I possess the gift of observation. Few things escape my notice."

"Is that so?" Christine asked, finding the young viscount unexpectedly entertaining. "What else have you observed?"

"You're not looking for a husband," he said without preamble, his eyes holding hers, waiting, observing.

Seeing no judgement on his face, Christine nodded. "You would be right to assume that."

"Your parents, however, disagree with your outlook on this issue."

Christine chuckled. "No great skill of observation is necessary to know that. I dare you to find parents who are delighted with their child's wish to remain unmarried."

Lord Eastwood laughed, a delighted twinkle in his startling blue eyes. "You are indeed correct. Maybe you will allow me to prove my skill to you in the future."

Nodding her head in agreement, Christine spent most of the evening in the viscount's company. He was a truly delightful man, who spoke his mind and who obviously shared her views with regard to marriage. Would he agree to her proposal? She wondered. Would she want him to?

Clearing her throat of the lump of embarrassment that had settled there, Christine pushed those thoughts away. Nothing had to be decided that very night. She would simply wait and see what happened. Maybe he was the very man who would help her forget about Wesley.

16

LADY RIGSBY'S PROPOSAL

*A*lthough he had all but wanted to run after Christine's carriage as it slowly made its way down the drive of Harrington Park, Wesley had remained behind, forcing himself to prolong his stay at his family's estate for as long as he could. January was already drawing to a close when he finally made his way to London.

Knowing that it would not serve him to shut himself away from society, Wesley reluctantly accepted an invitation to a ball. Would Christine be there? It was the only question on his mind as the carriage pulled to a stop outside the massive townhouse.

Climbing the steps, Wesley felt his heart hammering in his chest as anticipation threatened to squeeze the air from his lungs. Bright lights stung his eyes as he proceeded through the throng of people, craning his head without being too obvious, which, of course, was doomed to be a failed attempt.

As he ventured from room to room, Wesley's heart began to slow for it seemed as though she was not among the attending guests. Just when he was about to reach for a glass of wine, he spotted her across the room, and his hand froze mid-air.

His throat closed up, and his knees almost buckled as he found the woman he…loved dancing with Lord Eastwood, one of London's most notorious rakes.

Her eyes glowed as she laughed at something Eastwood had said, his gaze running over her in a way that made Wesley's stomach turn. Christine couldn't possibly be aware of her dance partner's reputation, could she?

A block of ice settled in Wesley's stomach as he realised his mistake. Of course, she was aware of the man's reputation. How could she not be? His reputation was in all likelihood the very reason she was dancing with him to begin with. After all, he would be the very man who would not hesitate to accept her proposal.

Eyes glued to the dancing couple, Wesley stood by the dance floor, forcing his stomach not to expel the food he'd eaten earlier.

When the music finally ended and Eastwood led Christine off the dance floor, their eyes met.

Her mind still buzzing with the dance and the music, Christine smiled at Lord Eastwood as he offered her his hand. "Would you care for a refreshment?" he asked, a smirk on his face. "I admit I quite long for one after such a strenuous activity."

Nodding her head in agreement, Christine couldn't help but notice how Lord Eastwood continually insinuated an intimate relationship between them. By now, there was not a doubt in her mind that he would accept her proposal should she choose to offer it.

As they ventured toward the refreshment table, Christine's eyes swept the crowd as though out of habit until to her utter shock, she found a familiar pair of blue eyes staring back at her.

The realisation that after all this time he was here hit her like a punch in the belly, and she almost toppled over.

It had to have shown on her face for the pain that had rested in his eyes only a moment ago vanished, replaced by concern. Instantly, he started toward her, but then stopped himself, his eyes shifting to the man beside her.

Embarrassed as though she was doing something wrong, Christine averted her gaze and followed Lord Eastwood to the refreshment table. There, she almost gulped down the glass of wine he handed her, desperate to steady her nerves.

Amused, Lord Eastwood looked at her. "Once again, you seem distracted...and rather rattled if you don't mind my saying. Is something the matter?"

Shaking her head, Christine returned her glass to the table. "Not at all. I was just...distracted," she ended lamely, knowing there was no way for her to explain.

"I see," Lord Eastwood said, a calculating sparkle in his eyes. "Do I dare ask if there is another gentleman whose company you would prefer to mine?"

Surprised by his boldness, Christine smiled, feeling a little of the tension leave her body. "You are indeed observant, my lord."

"Ouch!" Lord Eastwood clutched his chest as though she had wounded him, thereby reminding her of the antics of another gentleman, who had never failed to make her laugh.

Sighing, Christine forced herself to ignore the memories that resurfaced and focus her attention on the man before her. He, at least, would not refuse her.

Although his insides ached, Wesley found himself unable to leave. He knew he ought to, and yet, he couldn't. He stayed long past midnight, watching the woman he loved exchange meaningful glances with Eastwood.

When Wesley finally fell into bed that night, his dreams tortured him with images that he had forced from his mind before. Had she already made good on her threat? Had she taken Eastwood as a lover?

The next few days passed in a blur until yet another invitation found its way to his townhouse. As he stared at the sweeping letters, Wesley could not bring himself to tear up the invitation and continue his life regardless of what Christine did.

Without a doubt, he knew she would be at the ball, and although he knew he ought to, he couldn't stay away. Torturous curiosity drew him there that night, and once again, he spent the better part of the night watching Christine and Eastwood as he himself stood half-hidden behind a towering column like a thief in a dark alley waiting for the opportune moment.

However, such a moment would never come.

"You seem quite forlorn?"

Almost spinning on his heel, Wesley found himself staring at Lady Rigsby, her clear blue eyes assessing the situation within a heartbeat as they shifted from him to Christine and Eastwood before returning to him once more. "However, it is quite obvious what has you looking so distraught."

His jaw clenched, Wesley was at a loss. After all, Lady Rigsby was far from a confidante, with whom he might find himself inclined to share such intimate knowledge. Over the years, they had exchanged a few polite words here and there. However, ever since her husband had passed on, London had seen very little of the young widow. "Are you closely acquainted with Miss Dansby?" he finally asked, hoping to steer the conversation away from his current emotional state.

Lady Rigsby smiled, then shook her head. "Not at all." Her eyes lingered on his face before she swallowed and dropped her gaze as though caught unawares by emotions she had long sought dead.

"Are you all right?" Wesley asked as her beautiful eyes clouded with sadness.

Pressing her lips together, she forced her mouth into a smile, then met his eyes. "You remind me of my late husband," she whispered, a slight catch in her voice. "You look at her the way he used to look at me." She took a slow breath. "It's been so long, I thought I'd handle it better. I apologise."

When she was about to turn away, Wesley stopped her. "I'm sorry for your loss," he said. "I didn't realise…I…" Straightening his shoulders, he smiled at her. "Would you care for a drink?"

A soft smile on her face, she nodded. "I would. Thank you."

After procuring a drink, they strolled around the ballroom, and quite unexpectedly, Wesley felt his own misery less acutely. "I barely knew your late husband," he said, hoping his words would not upset her, "but from what I heard he was a good man."

Swallowing, she nodded. "He was."

"I apologise for reminding you of him. I assure you it was not my intention."

Lady Rigsby chuckled. "Neither did I mean to intrude," she said, her eyes shifting to someone beyond his shoulder. "I suppose something in the way you looked at her drew me near."

Drawing a deep breath, Wesley forced himself not to turn his head and look at Christine.

"Did she refuse you?" Lady Rigsby asked bluntly.

Somewhat surprised, Wesley nodded. "She did."

"Why?" Lady Rigsby asked, once more glancing past him. "She clearly cares for you. Her eyes have been shooting daggers at me ever since we started speaking."

Wesley's own eyes bulged. "She...what?" Unable to help himself, he spun around, his eyes finding Christine as though they were two magnets inevitably drawn to one another.

The moment he caught her staring, she quickly dropped her gaze, however, not before he had seen something that also burned in his own heart whenever he saw her with Eastwood: jealousy.

Wesley's heart skipped a beat, and it took all of his willpower not to stride across the room and steal her away.

"Why did she refuse you if you don't mind my prying?"

"Because she doesn't believe in marriage," Wesley admitted, forcing his eyes away from Christine. "However, I cannot...I would not..."

Lady Rigsby nodded. "I see. That is quite honourable of you." Once more, her eyes shifted to the dancing couples, and a thoughtful expression came to her face before her gaze returned to him. "The tragedy of your situation pains me greatly," she whispered, then leaned closer conspiratorially. "Please allow me to help you."

Wesley frowned, a sliver of hope pulsing in his chest. "How?"

A soft curl came to Lady Rigsby's lips before she coyly dropped her gaze for a moment. "Pretend she doesn't exist," she whispered to him as though they were sharing intimate secrets. "Pretend you care about me the way you care about her."

Somewhat confused, Wesley frowned.

"It'll help her realise what she is risking by refusing your offer," Lady Rigsby explained. "Believe me, if she truly loves you, she will not be able to stand by as you..." She raised her eyebrows meaningfully, and Wesley's eyes widened in shock.

A soft laugh escaped her before she shook her head. "Do not worry. I have no intention of seducing you. I merely hope to unite two people who so very obviously belong together." Again, she took a slow breath as though needing to steady her nerves. "Will you let me help?"

Seeing the pain and anguish in her eyes at the memory of her beloved husband, Wesley nodded gratefully, touched by her selflessness.

"Ask me to dance," Lady Rigsby whispered. "And try not to look at her. Only look at me."

17

A TRULY LUCKY MAN

Shocked beyond imagining, Christine stared as Wesley led the young widow onto the dance floor. As shaken as he had seemed before when their eyes had met as disinterested did he appear now, his eyes gazing almost lovingly down at the beautiful lady in his arms as they twirled around the room to the soft melody of a waltz.

"Would you care for a stroll?" Lord Eastwood asked, his eyes showing her a deeper meaning than his words would have suggested.

Christine took a slow breath, willing her hammering heart to slow down as the world began to blur before her eyes. She needed to think. This could not be happening! What *was* happening? How could he...? What...? When...?

All the times that she had refused Wesley's proposal, threatening to invite another man into her bed if he was not interested, she had never once contemplated the idea of him with another woman. How foolish of her! How could she not have seen this coming?

"No," she finally said, "I'd rather rest my feet for a little while. Would you be so kind as to fetch me another drink?"

With a slight nod of his head and a devilish sparkle in his eyes, Lord Eastwood marched off.

Instantly, Christine shifted her full attention back to the couple on the dance floor. Was this how Wesley had felt seeing her with Lord Eastwood? Finally, she understood his pained expression, wondering what her own face looked like in that very moment.

When the music ended, Christine breathed a sigh of relief as the young couple instantly broke apart, each venturing in the opposite direction as the other. Exchanging a few words here and there, Lady Rigsby eased closer to the side door, glanced around and then quickly slipped out.

Frowning, Christine looked around for Wesley, who stood by the refreshment table, gulping down another glass of wine, his eyes fixed on the very door Lady Rigsby had just disappeared through.

Oh, he wouldn't! Christine thought, hoped, tried to convince herself when Wesley suddenly set down the glass and made for the door with determination in his eyes.

In the very moment when Christine thought she would go mad, Lord Eastwood reappeared by her side, holding out a glass of wine to her.

Turning her head to look at him, Christine couldn't help but stare at the glass and then at Eastwood. What was she doing? This man didn't care about her. He merely wanted to...

Christine swallowed. Finally, she understood what Wesley had tried to make her see. To Eastwood, she was just one woman of many. To Wesley, she was the one.

Or she had been.

As her heart hammered in her chest, threatening to break her ribcage, Christine spun around, eyes frantically searching for the man who held her heart.

Only, he was nowhere to be seen.

Was she too late? Had he already disappeared through the door and gone after Lady Rigsby?

"Is something wrong?" Lord Eastwood asked, a hint of annoyance in his voice.

Ignoring him as well as the glass he was still holding out to her, Christine fled the ballroom. Willing her feet to keep from running, she slipped out into the hall, eyes searching for a sign as to where they had gone. She peeked into one room after another before tell-tale sounds reached her ears.

Oh, if this woman so much as laid a finger on him, she'd kill her on the spot!

Following the widow's soft giggle down the hall, Christine forced herself to remain calm. Stopping outside a door left ajar, she took a deep breath, then slowly pushed open said door and…her jaw dropped open as she found Wesley standing with his back to her, Lady Rigsby in his arms.

Instantly, her eyes narrowed and her jaw clenched as murderous thoughts raced through her head. Unable to control herself, Christine stormed toward them. "Get your hands off him! He's mine!"

Standing with his back to the door was torture as they listened for Christine's approaching footsteps. Would she come? Would the thought of him with another woman upset her as much as the thought of her with another man upset him? He could only hope so.

"She's coming," Lady Rigsby whispered in his ear, and he tensed as she slid her arms around his neck. This didn't feel right.

About to step back, Wesley heard the slight draft of air as the door slid open followed by a moment of stunned silence that almost drove him mad before angry footsteps stormed toward them. "Get your hands off him!" Christine snarled. "He's mine!"

At her words, Wesley thought he would faint with joy. However, reminding himself not to give in too soon, he forced his features back under control. Lifting his head, he turned around, eyes disinterested as he beheld the snarl on her face and the fire burning in her eyes.

"What are you doing here?" he asked before he glanced at Lady Rigsby as though in apology.

Jaw clenched, Christine fumed. "I…I…was looking for you." A tinge of red rose to her cheeks as her anger slowly wore off and embarrassment found her.

"Why?" Wesley asked, taking a step forward. "What is it to you what I do or who I am with? After all, you've made your feelings perfectly clear."

Snorting, Christine shook her head, sadness coming to her eyes, eyes that suddenly brimmed with tears. "I see. Well, if you've already turned your attention elsewhere, then whatever there was between us clearly was of very little consequence." Turning on her heel, she made for the door.

However, before Wesley could even take a step to stop her, Lady Rigsby came forward. "Wait!" she called, then stepped around him and toward Christine, who reluctantly turned back to face them.

"Why?" Christine asked, disgust in her eyes as she looked at Lady Rigsby. "So you can parade your triumph under my nose?"

Lady Rigsby took a slow breath. "I did indeed triumph," she said, kindness ringing in her voice that put a frown on Christine's face. "The moment I saw you, I knew you belonged together. He is yours. Never doubt that."

Through narrowed eyes, Christine looked at the woman before her. "It was not real?" Then her eyes shifted to Wesley. "You tricked me?"

Lady Rigsby shook her head. "No, we showed you how you truly feel." Then she glanced at Wesley before returning her eyes to Christine. "Nothing happened. I swear it."

Christine nodded, jaw trembling as though she was about to cry…or lash out at someone in anger.

"Be good to each other," Lady Rigsby implored them, and Wesley could see the sadness that engulfed her. From the bottom of his heart, he hoped that one day she would find happiness again.

After the door had closed behind the young widow, Wesley and Christine stood across from each other like two strangers, barely daring to look the other in the eye. Too much had happened, too much had been revealed, and yet, doubt still hung in the air like a thick fog.

Glancing at Christine, Wesley took a deep breath. Never had he seen her so shaken up. She was always so calm and collected, confident in every way. Now, she looked nothing like the woman he knew, and he realised how frightening all this had to be for her. "What do you want?" he asked, taking a step toward her.

Lifting her eyes off the floor, she met his gaze. "I…Well…"

Willing to reach out to her one last time, Wesley walked up to her and took her cold hands in his. "I want you," he whispered, forcing himself not to look away. "I always have–although in the beginning I didn't know it. I didn't want to know it. Believe me, this isn't easy for me, either." He swallowed as she looked up at him, her lower lip quivering in anticipation. "I love you."

A deep smile spread over her face, and for a moment, she dropped her gaze.

"You're the one woman I can actually see myself spending the rest of my life with. I know that marriage frightens you, but I promise that I won't promise you anything I will not keep."

An amused smile curled up her lips, and the muscles in her jaw relaxed.

"If it makes you happy, I will not promise to do anything *until death do us part*," he said lightly, sensing that the mood was slowly shifting. "We don't have to be perfect. Nothing is. If you wait for perfect, you'll be waiting your whole life because it doesn't exist." Sliding a hand along the side of her jaw, he cupped her cheek. "However, in my humble opinion, what we have is frighteningly close to perfect."

"It is." Nodding, Christine met his gaze. "I love you, too."

All air escaped Wesley's lungs in one gigantic sigh of relief, and his eyes closed to savour the moment.

"You didn't know?" Christine asked, a frown marking her face as she looked up at him.

"How could I know?" Wesley snorted. "I can't even count how many times you refused to marry me, and I don't want to count how often you threatened to take a lover." A shiver went over him, and he quickly shrugged off that unbearable thought.

Then he stopped, and his heart twisted in his chest. "You didn't...?" Staring into her eyes, he swallowed. "I mean, you and Eastwood didn't...?"

"No, we didn't." Delight came to her eyes as she looked into his. "You truly love me, don't you?"

Relieved, Wesley drew her closer. "Why would that surprise you?"

"I don't know." Christine shrugged. "I just never saw myself as...as a wife. I don't know if I can be."

A delighted smile came to Wesley's face. "Are you accepting my proposal?"

Frowning, Christine sighed, a hint of disappointment edged in her eyes. "To tell you the truth, I had my heart set on taking a lover. It's such a rebellious notion for a woman, and I've always seen myself as a bit of a rebel."

124

Wesley laughed. "Well, then I propose the following: I'll accept your proposal tonight," her eyes widened, and the corners of her mouth curled into a smile, "if you'll accept mine in the morning." To underline his words, Wesley tightened his arms around her and his head dipped down, placing a gentle kiss on her lips.

"Tonight?" Christine whispered against his lips as her arms rose and came around his neck.

Wesley nodded. "I'll be your lover tonight and your husband...well, fiancé in the morning."

"That sounds promising."

"Agreed then?"

"Agreed."

The second the word left her lips, Wesley kissed her the way he had wanted to for a long time. Lost in each other's arms, they forgot the world around them and were only reminded of where they were when the sound of footsteps hastening down the hall echoed to their ears.

"We should leave," Wesley whispered once the threat had left. "I'll call for the carriage. Meet me by the entrance." Then he stopped. "What about your parents?"

Christine shrugged. "I'll speak to my mother."

"What will you tell her?"

"The truth, of course."

Wesley's eyes opened wide. "And you don't think she'll object?"

"She won't object if it means I end up a married woman. After all, I'm not a young debutante who loses her heart to every man who smiles at her. I know what I want, and I'm not easily persuaded."

Wesley chuckled. "I can attest to that. You truly are one of a kind."

Before she slipped out the door, Christine smiled back at him. "You're a lucky man, Wesley Everett. A truly lucky man."

Taking a deep breath, Wesley rubbed his hands over his face. It had been a long night. More than that, it had been a few terribly long and trying couple of weeks. However, in the end, his brother had been right. When it came to love, nothing was impossible.

EPILOGUE

Harrington Park, March 1819

Standing in front of the large window opening her bedchamber to the gardens below, Christine gazed out at the starlit night. The moon shone in all its splendour, its reflection dancing over the silent water of the large fountain. It was a peaceful sight, and Christine willed it to calm her own rattled nerves.

Two months had passed since she had accepted Wesley's proposal, and in another two months she would be his wife. And yet, few things had been settled with regard to her wedding as their attention had been directed elsewhere.

After their first night together, they had shared their news with their families and then immediately returned to Harrington Park. It had been a compromise. Only here were they able to spend the nights under the same roof without raising people's suspicions and causing a scandal, for Catherine and William had generously agreed to remain at Harrington Park during the first few months of the new Season…in order to give them an alibi.

Wesley had insisted on it for he was still concerned about her reputation and could not bear the thought of his fiancée being slandered behind her back.

As though speaking…or thinking of the devil conjured him, the door to her room opened and Wesley strode in, a beaming smile on his face. "I apologise for missing supper, but I have wonderful news." Seeing her face, he stopped. "Is something wrong?"

Christine sighed. "I thought planning a wedding would be fun, but somehow it's not."

"Why?" Coming toward her, he held open his arms and she stepped into his embrace, resting her head on his shoulder.

"Because although *I* am the bride," she said, a tinge of anger in her voice, "apparently everyone has an opinion about…everything." Straightening, she looked up. "Honestly, was I this bad when Catherine got married? Tell me, please."

A smirk came to his face, and his eyes shifted from hers.

"You cannot be serious!" she snapped, stepping back and slapping him on the arm. "Why would you say such a thing?"

His eyebrows rose. "I didn't say anything!"

"Well, you might as well have!" Hands on her hips, she strode back toward the window, drawing a deep breath into her lungs. "Maybe we should just elope."

"That sounds tempting," Wesley whispered in her ear as he came to stand behind her, his arms coming around her waist, pulling her close. "How soon can you be packed?"

Despite her intention of maintaining her more than justified anger about the intrusion of her female relatives with regard to her wedding plans, Christine chuckled and leaned back against him, feeling herself relax. "They would never forgive us."

"To hell with them," Wesley mumbled, kissing her neck.

Although his suggestion had only been in jest, Christine felt tempted to accept, and yet, she knew that she would end up regretting not sharing her wedding day with her sister and the rest of their families. "They are a part of us," she whispered. "As exhausting as they are, I wouldn't know what to do without them." She took a deep breath, enjoying her fiancé's caresses, when a frown came to her face. "Didn't you say you had good news?"

"No," he mumbled into her hair, "I said I had wonderful news."

Turning around, Christine looked up at him expectantly. "Do you want me to guess?"

Wesley chuckled. "I happened to meet Lord Fythe today."

A jolt went through Christine at the mention of Marianne's husband. With all that had been going on, they had rarely seen each other in the past few months, and although her wedding day was fast approaching, Christine was uncertain whether it would be the right place for them to renew their friendship. Especially considering that Marianne suspected her husband of infidelity. "And? Who did you see him with?"

"No one," Wesley said, a delighted smile on his lips. "He is not having an affair."

"What?" Frowning, Christine tried to remember her friend's words. "But Marianne said he'd become distant and that he lied about where he'd been."

"Well, I suppose that's true," Wesley said, his eyes sparkling with delight.

Christine huffed. "If you intend to draw this out any longer, Wesley Everett, I swear—"

"He's planning a surprise," Wesley interrupted her small outburst. "For their one-year anniversary."

Christine's eyes opened wide. "He is?"

Wesley nodded. "It's a journey to the continent."

"She's always wanted to go," Christine mused, surprised that Lord Fythe would be so thoughtful. He had always seemed rather indifferent.

"Do you now believe that not all husbands are evil?" Wesley mocked as his arms pulled her close once more.

"I never said that," Christine objected, trying to step back. His arms, however, held her tightly against him. "I simply have never been very fond of husbands."

A mischievous twinkle in his eyes, Wesley leaned closer. "Thank goodness I'm only your fiancé. Maybe we should postpone the wedding." Capturing her lips, he kissed her deeply. "Maybe we should cancel it altogether."

Before he could kiss her again, Christine turned her head. "Not after I fought your mother for over an hour about the flower arrangement," she gasped as his lips trailed down her neck. "You're mine, Wesley Everett, so you'd better make your peace with that."

Lifting his head, he looked into her eyes, a smile on his face. "That's the most wonderful threat I've ever heard. How could a man refuse?"

Returning his smile, Christine reached for him and pulled him back down to her before they stumbled backwards and fell onto the bed. "I'm demanding my pre-marital rights, Mr. Everett."

"I've never heard of those."

Grinning, she whispered in his ear. "I'll show you."

ABOUT BREE

USA Today bestselling author, Bree Wolf has always been a language enthusiast (though not a grammarian!) and is rarely found without a book in her hand or her fingers glued to a keyboard. Trying to find her way, she has taught English as a second language, traveled abroad and worked at a translation agency as well as a law firm in Ireland. She also spent loooong years obtaining a BA in English and Education and an MA in Specialized Translation while wishing she could simply be a writer. Although there is nothing simple about being a writer, her dreams have finally come true.

"A big thanks to my fairy godmother!"

Currently, Bree has found her new home in the historical romance genre, writing Regency novels and novellas. Enjoying the mix of fact and fiction, she occasionally feels like a puppet master (or mistress? Although that sounds weird!), forcing her characters into ever-new situations that will put their strength, their beliefs, their love to the test, hoping that in the end they will triumph and get the happily-ever-after we are all looking for.

If you're an avid reader, sign up for Bree's newsletter at www.breewolf.com as she has the tendency to simply give books away. Find out about freebies, giveaways as well as occasional advance reader copies and read before the book is even on the shelves!

Thank you very much for reading!

Bree

Rules to Be Broken

(#5 A Forbidden Love Novella Series)

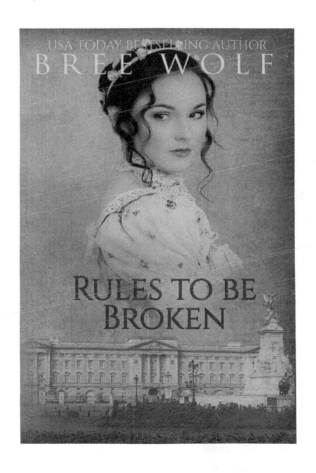

PROLOGUE

London, Summer 1815
Four Years Ago

er heart thudding in her chest, Diana tiptoed down the small cobblestone path as her dainty steps echoed through the night air. The moon shone overhead, casting its silvery light into the shadowy dark of the gardens, and from the terrace, the sounds of music and laughter reached her ears. The earl's ball was still in full swing, and to Diana's delight, it had been rather easy to escape her parents' watchful eyes and sneak out into the night.

A part of Diana's mind warned her, cautioned her that such a behaviour could have disastrous consequences. Her heart, however, was focused on one thing alone: the man she loved.

If she could only speak to him for a few moments and assure him that his pursuit was indeed most welcomed, he would surely speak to her father that very night and ask for her hand in marriage.

At the thought, the breath caught in her throat, and she stopped in her tracks. Drawing the fresh night air into her lungs, Diana sought to steady her nerves. When the slight dizziness that had seized her so unexpectedly finally subsided, she swallowed and then proceeded down the path.

In the dark, the tall-growing hedges and bushes looked ominous, and more than once, Diana drew back with a startled gasp because she feared she had stumbled upon someone lurking in the shadows, intent on doing her harm.

"Where is he?" she mumbled under her breath craning her neck, hoping to catch a glimpse of his tall, striking figure.

After he had asked her to follow him into the night—the gaze in his smoldering eyes saying more than a thousand words ever could—Diana had not hesitated. Ensuring that her parents were otherwise occupied, she had slipped out the terrace doors, following his silhouette until it had disappeared among the shadows.

As the chilled night air brushed over her heated cheeks, Diana's feet carried her onward until at last she found the small pavilion standing like an island in the midst of a green ocean, its tall, white-washed pillars reaching into the sky.

His back to her, he stood motionless on the other side of the small space, sheltered under a canopy roof, his strong arms resting on the small rail, and stared out into the night.

At the very sight of him, Diana's heart soared and a rush of emotions swept through her body. Her lips began to tingle at the mere thought of his mouth pressed to hers, and her palms grew moist with nervous anticipation.

Taking another deep breath, she stepped forward, her dainty steps all but silent as she approached him. His intoxicating scent mingled with the soft night smells as the jasmines began to bloom, and

Diana thought for a moment she would faint on the spot as her heart raced in her chest.

Coming to stand behind him, she lifted her hands, desperate to be in his arms, and softly placed them on the top of his back, gently letting them slide down over his strong muscles.

The moment Diana touched him, he froze before drawing in a deep breath. "I've been waiting for you," he whispered in that deep, raspy voice that made her breath catch in her throat every time it reached her ears.

A smile spread over her face, and joy filled her heart.

Like a feline, he suddenly spun around and pulled her into his arms, his hungry mouth seeking hers.

Locked in his tight embrace, Diana abandoned all thought as her body responded to his touch as though it recognized him from a previous life. Deep down, Diana had always known that he was her soul mate.

As his lips roamed hers, she held on to him, feeling her knees grow weak. A soft gasp escaped her as his hands travelled upward, and he suddenly drew back.

In the dim light of the moon, he gazed into her eyes, a slight frown curling his brows before he stepped back. "I apologise, Miss—"

"Diana!"

At the sound of her father's enraged voice, Diana's head spun around. Finding her parents standing by the tall-growing hedge that shielded the pavilion from passersby, she swallowed as their disbelieving eyes stared at them, shifting from her to the man by her side.

Turning to face her parents as they hurried toward them, their faces pale in the moonlight, Diana smiled, "Father, Mother, I can explain."

"I most certainly hope so," her father snapped, his sharp eyes travelling from her to her future husband. "Norwood, what is the meaning of this?"

Clearing his throat, Robert Dashwood stepped forward. "I apologise, Sir. There has been some misunderstanding. I—"

"Whatever misunderstanding you thought has occurred, I expect the next words I hear to include a proposal considering the liberties you've just now taken with my daughter!"

With love in her heart and a smile on her face, Diana turned to the man by her side. Butterflies fluttered in her belly as she took a deep breath. *This was it! The moment she had been waiting for her entire life.*

"A proposal?" Laughing, her soul mate shook his head. "I'm afraid I have to disappoint you."

Staring at him, Diana felt the blood rush from her cheeks as the world grew dim around her. "What?" she gasped, her knees suddenly weak as pudding as the butterflies in her belly died a slow death.

"I apologise," he said, his eyes shifting from her father to her. "As I said, this was a misunderstanding."

"A misunderstanding?" her father boomed as heart-wrenching sobs tore from Diana's throat, and she sank into her mother's arms. "You take advantage of a young girl, and then you refuse to do the only decent thing left. What kind of a gentleman are you?"

Chuckling, Robert Dashwood leaned against the rail. "The worst kind, I assure you."

"Social etiquette dictates that—"

"I don't care about social etiquette—"

"You will be ruined. Your reputation—"

"My reputation will not suffer for all of London already knows the kind of man I am." Standing up straight, the notorious viscount stepped forward, fixing her father with serious eyes. "Your daughter, on the other hand, has everything to lose. Therefore, I suggest you be reasonable."

"You downright refuse to marry her?" her father huffed.

"Yes, sir," he confirmed. "You will be well-advised to return to the festivities before we are discovered. No harm has been done so far."

Shaking his head, her father coughed, "No harm? You've compromised her."

"Upon my honour—or what is left of it—it was only a kiss."

Only a kiss? Diana's head spun as she clung to her mother, her hopes crashing into a black abyss that was threatening to swallow her whole. What was happening? Did he not love her? Had he not told her so a million times? Had his loving gaze not spoken the words that his lips had confirmed a mere few minutes ago?

Glaring at the man she loved, her father returned to her side. "You are without honour, Norwood. I sincerely hope that one day you will reap what you sow."

An amused smile on his face, Lord Norwood nodded to her father before his eyes dropped to hers. "All my best to you, Miss…Lawson, is it?" Then he turned and walked away, the shadows swallowing him whole as though he had never been there.

Supported by a parent on either side, Diana placed one step before the other, her mind tormented by the incomprehensibility of what had just happened and her heart aching with the love so unexpectedly ripped from her life.

"I can only hope that Norwood keeps quiet," her father mumbled under his breath, anger still ringing in his sharp voice. "If anyone finds out what happened here tonight, your chances for a favourable match will be ruined."

In that moment, Diana could not bring herself to care. After all, what value could her reputation possibly have when her heart had just been ripped into pieces?

A FORBIDDEN LOVE
NOVELLA SERIES

For more information, visit

www.breewolf.com

LOVE'S SECOND CHANCE SERIES

For more information, visit

www.breewolf.com